ADA'S

ADA'S HEART

•

Sandra Wilkins

AVALON BOOKS

NEW YORK

Published by Thomas Bouregy & Co., Inc.
160 Madison Avenue, New York, NY 10016

Library of Congress Info Cataloging-in-Publication
Wilkins, Sandra.
Ada's heart / Sandra Wilkins.
    p. cm.
ISBN 978-0-8034-9886-0 (hardcover : acid-free paper)
1. Actresses—Fiction. 2. Shawnee (Okla.)—History—20th
century—Fiction. I. Title.
PS3623.I5485A33   2008
813'.6—dc22   2007037597

PRINTED IN THE UNITED STATES OF AMERICA
ON ACID-FREE PAPER
BY HADDON CRAFTSMEN, BLOOMSBURG, PENNSYLVANIA

To Andy, Chloe, and Phoebe—all my love forever.

I am deeply indebted to Denise and Marsha. Your friendship was the spark for the story. God put us in the right place at the right time.

To Lisa P. and others from various writer's groups and conferences for the knowledge I gleaned from them.

To my husband, Andrew, for believing in my dream all these years. To Chloe and Phoebe for their unselfish love and joy.

To my parents, Dale and Janice, my brother, Michael, and other relatives for their support, encouragement, and willingness to answer all sorts of odd questions. I especially want to mention my grandmother, Vera James Broudrick, for her cheerful encouragement to keep writing stories when I was young. I know she's smiling down from heaven.

Chapter One

May 1905

"Next stop, Shawnee, Oklahoma Territory!" the conductor bellowed as he balanced his way down the aisle of the moving railroad car.

The passengers began to stir as the bells clanged, the whistle blew, and the large steam engine slowed. Ada Marsh closed the script she had been studying and tucked it into her tapestry valise. She glanced out the window. Through wind–whipped gray smoke and white steam from the train, she viewed the prospering frontier town for the first time.

The impressive Santa Fe Depot appeared to be standing guard over the modest clapboard homes

1

nearby. The newly erected tan rock depot looked like a small castle. A multiarched veranda curved around one side, meeting a circular tower that soared over the red clay-tiled roofline.

Ada was surprised at the size of the crowd gathered around the station, waving at the passengers on the train as it proceeded north. She wondered if the entire town knew of her arrival. She still felt a small thrill when people came to see her and her fellow performers. It always energized her when she was weary of traveling. She was curious about the people she would meet in this town. One of the things she enjoyed most about her profession was the opportunity it provided to encounter interesting characters.

She viewed her reflection in the window. She noted that she had chosen the perfect color of mahogany serge for her suit from that little shop in Fort Worth. It matched her hair perfectly. She pulled the long hat pin out of her large ebony hat and secured it more firmly in hopes it would not fly away in the brisk breeze. She put on her black kid gloves, and she tried to brush the wrinkles out of her skirt.

She nudged her dozing companion, lifting the black fedora off his face. Her fiancé, Hugh Wellington, reluctantly opened one ice blue eye.

"We're here," she said with a lilt in her voice.

His long legs were propped up on the seat across the way. He placed his low-cut boots on the floor and sat up from his lounging position. He passed long fingers through his raven hair, retrieved his hat, and returned it to his head. He ran a forefinger and thumb over his thin mustache.

"Another glorious frontier village." Sarcasm dripped from his clipped English accent as he flashed her a smile.

"Hush," she reprimanded.

"I will be on my best behavior, my darling Ada."

"You'd better be." She shook her head but could not help smiling at him.

She looked over her shoulder to confirm that the actors in her troupe were preparing to disembark. Some were dressed elegantly, others excessively, reflecting their personalities. Lisette was lovely, Myra impractical, Sara professional, and Dixie flamboyant. Paul was humorous, Tom serious, and her Hugh was . . . indescribable.

She secretly studied him as he unabashedly charmed a matronly woman across the aisle into promising she would attend their performance at the end of the week. Ada had known Hugh only three months. He was a big asset to the company, although he had not made a great impression on her at first. His self-confidence bordered on vanity, but he quickly won her over, as he did every audience that saw him. A whirlwind romance ended with their engagement two weeks ago.

He was impeccably dressed, as always. Even after a long train ride, he was not crumpled at all. He was in fine form in a black cutaway frock coat and an embroidered scarlet vest. He reclaimed his shiny black walking stick. He placed a manicured hand on the engraved gold knob, his pinkie ring sparkling in the sunlight.

The locomotive screeched into the depot. Everyone onboard was jarred as the train came to a stop. The troupe let the other passengers exit while they gathered their things.

"Well, my emerald-eyed jewel, are we ready?" Hugh inquired.

"Of course, darling." She grinned.

She picked up her valise and followed her friends down the aisle. One by one her company stepped down onto the brick paving and congregated nearby. As she emerged, the throng outside erupted into applause. She was taken aback by the welcome.

Hugh, with hand outstretched, gave her a low bow. His eyes twinkled as he said, "Your admirers await."

She beamed as she waved to the kind people. She took Hugh's hand as she descended. Shouts of regard came from the swarm as they respectfully parted for the actors and actresses to pass through. She clutched Hugh's arm as he escorted her.

A man with a serious countenance met them with hat in hand. He led them to the Norwood Hotel coach. As Ada waited to board, she noticed an earnest young woman trying to get close.

"Miss Marsh!" The woman raised a notepad. "Miss Marsh!" Her plain straw hat was knocked askew as she was jostled out of the way.

Hugh hopped into the hotel coach, taking the last seat. He reached for Ada. "I'm afraid this is the only seat remaining, darling." He motioned to his lap and gave her a devilish smile.

"Oh, you—" she squeaked as he pulled her down.

Everyone laughed as they squeezed in, silks and lace ruffles everywhere. Lisette was happily perched on Paul's knees, so Ada decided it would not be too scandalous to remain where she was.

"This is mad!" Dixie exclaimed as the conveyance pulled away from the station. "I've never seen such a crowd."

"The acclaim for my talent has preceded us," Paul jested. He ducked as various articles were flung in his direction, not at all bothered by the teasing.

Ada, in the meantime, was having difficulty breathing normally. Her heart always pounded when she was too close to Hugh. His cologne was as intoxicating as he was. He brushed his lips on her neck, and his mustache made her shiver. At twenty-seven, she thought she should be past these fanciful feelings. Hugh Wellington was a dangerous man to be near.

To try to distract herself, she peered out the window as they rode west down Main Street. Two- and three-story redbrick buildings lined the road. Some of the streets were even paved with red bricks. A few blocks later they turned north on Broadway. The five-story Norwood Hotel towered over the neighboring buildings. The carriage halted in front of the hotel, and they all poured out.

"How nice," Ada murmured as she paused to look up at the Norwood. Stone gargoyles graced the brick façade along the roofline. At the center of the second story, French doors were set into a large archway that led out to a balcony with wrought iron railings.

Hugh urged her forward, and they entered the lobby through glass doors under the balcony. He left her for a moment to check them in.

Ada wandered around and approved of their accommodations. A large restaurant and a barbershop were just off the large lobby. The wood floors gleamed, and chandeliers flickered from the ornate painted tin ceilings. It was a nice hotel for such a small city.

A commotion at the front door caught her attention.

A woman hurried in and skidded to a stop. She tried to straighten the hat on her thick brown hair as she scanned the room. She tugged on her black vest. She smiled triumphantly when she spotted Ada.

Ada recognized her as the young woman from the train station. She acknowledged her politely as she approached.

"Miss Marsh." She held out her hand. "I'm Gwen Sanders. I'm the society columnist for the *Shawnee Globe*."

Ada shook her hand. "I'm pleased to meet you."

"Oh, the pleasure is certainly mine," she gushed. "I saw you perform last year in Guthrie. You were marvelous."

"Thank you for your kindness." She smiled her pleasure. "Weren't you at the depot moments ago?"

Gwen laughed at herself and she motioned to a man and a young woman who had just entered the building. "My cousin, Luke, was good enough to rush my friend and me over here in his buggy."

Ada nodded graciously toward them. The man wore western clothes and a tan wool ranch hat. His rugged looks were framed by wayward brown hair. The young woman seemed to have a quiet way about her. She was dressed modestly in a white shirtwaist and light blue linen skirt. She was fair and blond with a heart-shaped face.

Ada turned her eyes back to the woman standing in front of her. Gwen's features were strong but pleasing. Her brown eyes were inquisitive as she observed the exuberant troupe at the front desk.

"Is there something I can do for you, Miss Sanders?" she asked, trying to steer the conversation back to the business at hand.

"I was hoping, Miss Marsh, that I could have an interview with you." Gwen held her pencil and notepad at the ready.

Hugh appeared at Ada's side, startling her. He took Ada's arm and tried to lead her away. "Miss Marsh has had a tiring journey. . . ."

"Oh, of course." Gwen began to back away. She blushed as she glanced at Hugh.

Ada frowned briefly at Hugh, and she moved from his grasp. She gave her full attention to Gwen. "Would luncheon tomorrow be agreeable, Miss Sanders?"

"Oh, yes."

"How about at one in the restaurant here?"

"That would be wonderful. Thank you so much, Miss Marsh. I'll see you then." She beamed and turned to leave.

"Oh, Miss Sanders, bring your friends if they would like to join us." She inclined her head toward the couple by the door.

"They will be thrilled." She pumped Ada's hand and dashed away.

After assuring they were alone, Ada faced Hugh. "Why were you so rude?" she hissed.

"I was rescuing you from that droll girl." He raised a dark eyebrow.

"This company and I did not get where we are by being impolite to the people we want to promote our troupe and *pay* to come see us." She pressed her lips together.

Conflicting emotions passed through his eyes until they finally appeared aloof. "Your point is taken, my dear."

Slightly embarrassed by the tone she had used, she tried to make amends. "Would you care to join me at the interview tomorrow?"

He put her hand into the crook of his arm. "I believe I would prefer to rehearse. I imagine Myra will accommodate me, since the leading lady will be otherwise occupied."

"I'm sure she wouldn't mind." Her understudy would jump at the chance to practice with the leading man. "But I will be there as soon as possible."

He gave her a knowing look. "I'm sure we will find some way to pass the time until you arrive."

"Oh, you insufferable—"

He cut her off with a kiss. "Truce?" he murmured.

"Truce," she whispered against his lips, not caring that several prominent citizens were scrutinizing their behavior.

He pulled away from her and winked. "I believe we've tantalized the public enough for today. Let's find our rooms." He led her toward the elevator. "I'm exhausted."

Chapter Two

"**I** don't know why I'm doin' this," Luke Logan muttered to his bay gelding, Samson, as he harnessed him to the covered buggy. "It's not like I don't have a thing better to do than gallivantin' around town."

He fastened the last buckle and lightly slapped Samson on the rump, sending dust flying. He climbed up to the buggy's cushioned front seat, picked up the reins, and urged the horse forward. He left the un-painted barn, driving past his simple white two-bedroom house down the long red dirt lane to the road.

He glanced back at his farm as he headed south. It was such a peaceful place. His house was built far from the road amid blackjack, red oak, and pecan

11

trees. Rock Creek ran east and west not far away. His fields were planted, and his herd of cattle was healthy and growing.

He had accomplished quite a bit in the last five years, and at thirty-two he felt settled. He shook his head. "And now I'm goin' with Gwen to have lunch with some actress," he mumbled. "I must be crazy." He smirked. "But then, Gwen could talk a pirate out of his peg leg."

His younger cousin, by seven years, had blossomed from an awkward girl into a persuasive and beautiful young woman. Last fall she had convinced her fiancé and her mother to let her move to Shawnee from Guthrie, the territorial capital. She wanted to be a writer. She found a position at one of the local newspapers. Her small column had grown into an interesting part of the *Globe*.

Of course, Luke had promised his Aunt Grace to watch out for Gwen. Which was why he was going back to town to keep an eye on things. Everyone knew that actors and actresses were a wild bunch. He wouldn't want Gwen and Rose to be unescorted around that slick actor fellow with the bit of a mustache. He didn't like the looks of him. He didn't know if he would be there or not, but he wasn't taking any chances.

He had to admit, though, he was more than curious

about Ada Marsh. Gwen had raved about her for weeks after she found out the Ada Marsh Players were coming to Shawnee. Miss Marsh was a fetching woman. He wondered what she was like underneath the surface. He guessed he would soon find out.

He snapped the reins on Samson's back to pick up the pace. He lived several miles north of Shawnee on Kickapoo Street. On a dry day it took a good thirty minutes to get to town. He usually didn't mind the solitude, but he was ready to see what this day would bring.

In due time, Luke made his way into Shawnee. He drove toward Park Street to pick up Rose. He smiled when he thought of Rose Dennis. She was a sweet young woman who had become fast friends with Gwen.

He had a sneaking suspicion that Gwen was trying to be a matchmaker. She had, supposedly in all innocence, suggested that he collect Rose first. He was flattered. He did like Rose, but the spark just wasn't there. He figured he might have to have a talk with Gwen before long.

He pulled up in front of the white picket fence at Mr. and Mrs. Dennis' handsome two-story cottage. Rose was sitting in a swing on the front porch. She waved at him and hurried down the walkway. She looked like spring in a shirtwaist of the palest pink.

Her light blond hair was piled loosely on the crown of her head, and a straw hat with pink ribbons and flowers was perched on top.

He got down as she neared. As he helped her up, he noticed that she even smelled like a rose. She settled into the plush backseat and arranged her skirts.

"How are you this fine day, Miss Dennis?" he inquired with a smile.

"Oh, I'm grand." Her pretty face flushed the brightest crimson, but her dark blue eyes lit up with excited anticipation. She clasped her gloved hands in her lap.

"Good, good." He sprang into the buggy, and they were soon off. "So, what do you think about going to see this actress?"

"It's exciting. It's difficult to believe someone so famous would come here."

"I know, but Shawnee's a bustlin' place. The three railroads comin' through have really helped business."

"We are growing quickly. We have a new large city hall, and the new Santa Fe Depot is really nice, and they're building a new library. . . ." She trailed off, apparently realizing how much she was talking.

"And don't forget the trolley," he added.

"Isn't it fun? You've ridden it, haven't you?" she asked.

"No. I haven't gotten around to it."

"Maybe you and I . . . and Gwen could ride it sometime?" she asked shyly.

He grinned over his shoulder at her. "You can count on it." He saw her turn red in the face before he went back to driving.

Luke turned onto Tenth Street and then down Market. He stopped in front of the large white three-story home that had been recently converted into a boardinghouse. The porch posts and shutters had a new coat of sky blue paint. He saw a curtain flutter at the window on the left side of the second floor, where Gwen's room was.

"Late again," he commented lightheartedly. He shook his head. "I wonder if she'll be late for her own wedding."

"Surely not. But I will be there—just in case," Rose said.

He twisted in his seat to face her. "When *are* they getting married?"

She shrugged. "I'm not sure. She wants to stay here a while longer, but I think Walter is ready for her to go back."

"I imagine. I don't believe I'd want my intended to move away from me," he admitted.

His words brought on an even more furious blush in Rose's cheeks. Even the tips of her small ears were dark pink. He tried to restrain a smile as he ducked his head and pulled down on the brim of his hat.

The front door of Mrs. Brown's boardinghouse slammed as Gwen raced down the steps faster than any lady should. She held the same straw hat to her head that she had worn the day before. She was dressed in a brown skirt, crisp white shirtwaist, and a black silk tie. She looked extremely professional. If only the world knew how funny that was.

Luke chuckled as Gwen handed him her notepad and pencil.

"What's so amusing, mister?" She shot him the evil eye as she helped herself up next to Rose.

"Oh, just reminiscin' about your dignified ways," he teased as the horse moved forward.

"What do you mean by that?" She sat up straighter in her seat.

"Seeing you rush down the walk like that reminded me of the time when we were still livin' in Kansas. You had stayed with us for the night. You ran through the cornfield in your nightgown, and it was torn to shreds by the time you got to your house on the other side."

Rose gasped. He peeked over his shoulder in time to see Gwen roll her eyes at him.

"I was only seven at the time, and that was your fault to begin with," she huffed. "You had me convinced that your pet cow had gone mad, and if she saw anything white, she would break free from her ropes. What else was I to do when I was on my way to the outhouse early that morning and found her staked out in front of it? My white gown was flapping in the breeze as I rounded the corner. I just kept on running. I wasn't about to wait to see how she was going to react."

Luke and Rose laughed.

"What about the time you showed up at church soakin' wet?" he asked playfully.

He saw Rose raise her eyebrows.

"As I recall, yet again that was your fault." She focused her attention on Rose. "It was a glorious spring day. Our parents agreed to let us leave early so we could walk off some of our energy on the way to church. I believe I was ten and Luke was a strapping seventeen."

He snickered, and she smacked him on the shoulder with the back of her hand.

"As I was saying, Luke said he knew a shortcut. So we took off through the fields and came to a creek probably ten feet wide. He had been there before and assured me we could cross by swinging over on a rope tied to this old tree."

"And?" There was a suspicious tone in Rose's voice.

"Well, my dear cousin grabs the rope and swings as pretty as you please, his gangly legs landing safely on the other side."

"Gangly?" he blustered.

"Hush. I'm telling this story. Anyway, he convinces me that I can do it too. He even says that he'll tell me when to let go of the rope so I would come to ground safe and secure. So, I get up my courage . . ."

"I don't recall it bein' that difficult to persuade you." He tried to look indignant.

Her eyes gleamed. "I worked up all my gumption, caught the rope, walked as far back as I could, and took off at a run. When I was half the way across, I heard him shout. I let go, and I splattered into the middle of the creek."

"Oh, no," Rose sympathized, but she tried to suppress a chuckle.

"I was madder than a hornet. So I just sat there in the water and cried."

"My brilliant idea didn't seem quite as funny then," he explained to Rose. "I tried and tried to coax her out, but she just sat there bawlin'. So I marched on in to help her out, and when—"

"When he bent over to help me up, I grabbed him by the ears and pulled him in too."

"You didn't!" Rose tittered.

"I did, I'm proud to say," Gwen gloated.

"What happened then?"

"We wrung ourselves out and went on to church," Luke stated.

"*He* thought we would be dry by the time we got there."

"I was . . . almost." He shrugged. "I learned my lesson, though. I thought my father and her mother would explode when they saw us. I couldn't sit for days after the tannin' I got."

"Me either. I don't think they ever believed it was all your fault. I'm surprised Mother ever trusted me with you again."

"Don't you believe her, Rose, that she was a little innocent," he said, turning to them. "She got me into a few messes."

"No." Gwen put a hand to her chest and tried, unsuccessfully, to appear appalled.

Luke shook his head at her. He parked the buggy near the hotel and set the brake. He rotated slowly and narrowed an eye at Gwen. "Does the name Gertrude James ring a bell?"

Gwen hooted and slapped her knee. "I'd forgotten all about that."

He puffed up. "Well, I certainly haven't." He pointed a thumb at Gwen while turning to Rose. "A year after the creek incident, our families were at a church picnic. The church ladies were raisin' money with a pie auction. Miss High-and-Mighty here told me that Miss James had baked a gooseberry pie and that she would like to share it with me."

Gwen sniggered.

"Seein' that gooseberry is my favorite, and Gertrude was a pretty black-haired little thing with a heart-stoppin' smile, I decided to bid on that pie. This other fella, Mel, and I were havin' a time of it. I think the bid was over a dollar when I noticed that Gertrude frowned every time I put my hand up. Her chin was even beginnin' to tremble. Then, out of the corner of my eye, I saw Gwen hee-hawin'."

"You didn't," Rose said to Gwen.

"She did. With my hand in midair, I figured out she had duped me. Poor Mel couldn't bid any higher, so I won the pie. Mel looked as if he wanted to choke me, and Gertrude was on the verge of tears."

"What did you do?" Rose asked with wide eyes.

"I did the honorable thing and gave the pie to them to enjoy." He wagged his head. "I don't know which hurt more—losin' the girl or the pie."

"Poor Luke." Gwen laughed as she hopped down from the buggy and retrieved her notebook and pencil. "I hear they have gooseberry pie at the hotel restaurant. I'll buy you a piece."

He grinned. "You can count on it, cousin." He descended and put up a hand to assist Rose to the ground. "Well, Rose, are you ready to dine with two miscreants and an actress?"

Her face was as bright as a new penny. "I wouldn't miss it."

He escorted them to the doors of the Norwood. They paused outside.

"Thank you both for coming," Gwen said as she adjusted her tie. "I *was* a tad nervous."

"We're glad to come." He opened the large door. "And we're proud of you."

She gave him a grateful look. The trio walked into the lobby. Miss Marsh wasn't there, so they went on into the restaurant.

Miss Marsh was sitting by the huge plate-glass window, stirring her coffee. Soft sunlight filtered in. Her luxuriant hair was done up in a full coiffure with a knot on top, and it sparkled with red and gold highlights. She was wearing a silk lavender shirt-waist stitched with black embroidery and a black taffeta skirt.

"Good heavens," Gwen whispered.

"How lovely," Rose added.

Luke silently agreed. She was prettier than any picture he had ever seen. She sat there confidently without seeming vain. She was a sight to behold.

He cleared his throat. "Let's go in."

They approached her table. She looked up at them

with strikingly green eyes. Her complexion was so pale, he could faintly see the blue veins in her long, slender neck. Her full lips parted as she smiled at them. She stood, and a soft, powdery scent wafted toward him. She offered her hand as Gwen introduced Rose.

Luke somehow remembered to remove his hat. He absently brushed his hair off his forehead while waiting for Gwen to present him.

"And, this is my cousin, Luke Logan."

Miss Marsh looked him straight in the eye as she placed her small hand in his. "I'm happy to make your acquaintance."

His heart flip-flopped when he heard her low, sultry voice. With all sincerity he said gently, "I'm glad to meet you."

Chapter Three

As Ada took her seat, Mr. Logan pushed the chair in for her. The young women sat across from her, leaving the space next to her for Mr. Logan.

She was relieved when they were seated. She had never thought of herself as being particularly delicate, but both Miss Sanders and Mr. Logan towered over her. She liked to have control over interviews, and she felt on the same level once they were all in their chairs.

"Thank you again for granting me an interview, Miss Marsh, and for inviting Rose and Luke. It was so gracious of you," Gwen said with candor.

Ada waved a hand. "Think nothing of it."

They chatted about the weather, Mr. Logan's farm,

and other niceties while the waitress took their orders and brought their drinks. Ada was amused when the strong, rugged man at her side poured cream and sugar into his coffee.

This farmer was so unlike the men she knew, including Hugh. His presence was powerful, and it made her uncomfortable. She had a difficult time following the conversation as she compared him to her fiancé. Mr. Logan's features were nearly too chiseled, his skin was almost too tan, and a vertical scar trailed through his right eyebrow. He didn't use any pomade, so his hair fell across his brow. His eyes were the color of molasses and seemed remarkably observant. He wore plain clothes, and he smelled wholesomely of dust and leather.

Ada reached for her coffee, hoping the aroma and a sip would clear her head.

"I thought we could begin before the food arrives." Gwen flipped open her notebook.

"Certainly," Ada agreed, glad to put her mind to other matters.

"First of all, I thought you were brilliant last year in Guthrie when I saw you in *Camille*. I don't think there was a dry eye in the house."

She smiled warmly. "That was a good run."

"What are you performing this time?"

"It's an original production written by Hugh

Wellington and Paul Freemont, two of our most popular actors. The play is quite humorous and romantic. We had our first showing in Fort Worth, Texas, and it was well received."

"Mr. Wellington is the newest member of your troupe?" Gwen asked as she scribbled without looking up.

"Yes, he has been with us a short time, but he is a great contributor already."

Gwen's efficient demeanor dropped for a moment as she leaned forward. "Was he the man who came up to us when we were speaking yesterday?"

"Yes, and he wishes to apologize if he seemed rude. He was seeing after my welfare." She cringed inwardly at fibbing, but she didn't want to hurt the earnest woman in front of her.

"Oh, I didn't even notice. I couldn't believe I was actually speaking to someone that handsome." She grinned. "There's a rumor around that you and Mr. Wellington are more than fellow actors. . . ." She whispered knowingly.

Ada chuckled. "You could say that. We became betrothed recently." She could have sworn Mr. Logan stiffened as she spoke.

"Congratulations." Gwen's pencil was poised in midair. "Do you mind if I print that?"

"You may."

"Fantastic. What a story this'll be." She wrote again. "Now, what about your background? Where are you from?"

"My parents died in an influenza epidemic when I was a small child. I was raised in St. Louis by my grandmother," she stated matter-of-factly.

There was sympathy in Gwen's brown eyes. "What made you want to become an actress?"

"My grandmother passed when I was sixteen. Becoming an actress to earn my keep seemed a little more glamorous than being a seamstress." She ran a forefinger over the crease in her linen napkin. "My grandmother sewed costumes for one of the theaters in St. Louis. I was always fascinated by the gaudy, sparkling clothes. Mrs. Martin, who owned the theater, took pity on me and let me give it a try. To both our surprises, I was good." She smiled.

"Mrs. Martin let me live in a tiny flat above the theater rather inexpensively. I took up designing and sewing the costumes to earn extra money. I saved every penny. Not necessarily because I was a miser, though. I was on my own quite young, after all, and I always wanted to be prepared for whatever might come my way." She took a sip of her coffee.

"What made you leave that situation?" Gwen asked.

"After six or so years, there was a small fire at the theater, and Mrs. Martin decided not to rebuild. The other regular actors and I were out of work, and I was out of a home, so we decided to form a traveling company, backed with my savings. Some of the other actors have come and gone, but I've been on the road ever since."

"I can't imagine having the fortitude to do such a thing." Rose spoke for the first time.

"Well, it was either nerve or stupidity. I haven't decided yet."

"Are you saying that you don't enjoy—" Gwen began.

"No, no. I do enjoy my profession. It is a difficult, isolating life, though. No friends except your fellow actors. Living in one hotel after the next." She glanced out the window and watched the people going about their business. "It's difficult to explain. Every city begins to look like the last. You begin to feel you have no home, no refuge."

"Because of that, do you plan to continue to act after your marriage?"

Ada was taken aback by Gwen's query. It hadn't occurred to her to stop working. Why couldn't she settle somewhere and finally have a home of her own? She must speak to Hugh about that.

"Miss Marsh?" Gwen inquired.

Ada gave her an impish grin. "I don't believe I will answer that question at this time."

Gwen nodded in understanding.

Two waitresses interrupted as they arrived with hot plates and bowls of food. Gwen put her open notebook and pencil aside. The waitresses curtsied before excusing themselves.

"That was odd," Gwen said after they scurried away. She scanned the room. Most of the patrons were whispering excitedly among themselves and watching their table. "Oh. . . ." She bent toward Ada. "You've been so friendly, I'd forgotten we were dining with a famous actress."

"For a moment it did feel as if we were only new acquaintances enjoying lunch." Ada glanced at the other customers and returned her gaze to her tablemates. "So, how does it feel to be the center of attention?"

"Strange," Gwen offered.

"Embarrassing," Rose murmured.

"Like a goldfish in a bowl with a scrawny cat sittin' on the rim," Luke said dryly.

She laughed at his evaluation. "Exactly, Mr. Logan, and I've been too close to those claws myself."

A stunning woman suddenly caused a commotion with her entrance. A table was hastily cleared for her. She sat with a flourish of her red silk gown. Luke inclined his head toward her. "Then I'd stay away from that one. She lives here at the hotel. She wouldn't think twice about scratching you with her claws."

"Oh, really?" Ada observed the woman with flowing black hair, whose dark eyebrows were drawn together as she watched Ada and her companions.

"That's Lilith Carlisle, the local celebrity," Gwen informed her. "Her next play was postponed because you were able to come. She's good, but she's not you."

"She's a flirt and a gossip," Luke said gruffly as he stabbed his fork into his mashed potatoes.

"She caused Luke all sorts of problems this winter." Rose gazed at him for the briefest moment before eating a bite of her stew.

"She had the whole town waggin' their tongues," he fumed.

"She insinuated that she and Luke were partaking in some . . . intimate activities." Gwen gave him a sorrowful look.

The muscles in his jaw tightened as he ground out, "I had only met her once. She didn't take it too well that I turned down her invitation to join her in her rooms. So she went and made up some story about me. I was never alone with her."

"We know." Rose spoke quietly.

Ada watched Lilith Carlisle's haughty expression turn into a scowl as she continued to watch them. "What happened after all of that?" she asked.

"The new banker came to town, and she moved on to him." He stared at Lilith with smoldering eyes.

"Are you sure she has moved on?" Ada asked with a raised eyebrow. "She appears to be a bit envious." She placed a hand over his sturdy one and tilted toward him with a mischievous expression. "Shall we see how good of an actor you are, and give her something to chafe about?"

His steely eyes softened, and his good humor returned. "I don't believe so, Miss Marsh. I wouldn't want to damage my glowin' reputation."

The pressure from his fingers was fleeting yet strong before she removed her hand. The corners of her mouth curved up. "I wouldn't want to sully your character, Mr. Logan," she teased.

"I appreciate that." His good mood seemed restored.

To hide her emotions, Ada turned back to her chicken and dumpling soup. She didn't know why she had done such a thing. Or why she even cared to help him.

"So, how long are you staying in Shawnee, Miss Marsh?" Rose asked. Her face was flushed as her eyes traveled between Ada and Luke. It was obvious that Miss Dennis had feelings for Mr. Logan.

What had she done now? If she had noticed earlier,

she wouldn't have touched him. She was in no way interested in him.

"We'll be leaving next Monday." She ate a bite.

"Good," Rose said evenly. "Perhaps you would care to join us for church services Sunday morning?"

Gwen and Luke started, apparently astonished by her bold behavior.

Ada cleared her throat "I appreciate the invitation, but the play is Saturday evening. We will be up until the wee hours of the morning."

Rose gave her a triumphant nod. Point made, she picked up her spoon. Her face was as red as a beet as she studied the contents of her bowl. Evidently she wasn't usually so assertive.

There was an awkward pause before Gwen gulped a mouthful of tea. "Will you be practicing all week?"

"Yes. We will rehearse every day. The others are all at the theater as we speak."

"I would love to see how the show is put together. Would you have time . . . ?"

"Miss Marsh is a busy woman, Gwen. I'm sure she doesn't have time to be escortin' us around." Luke's deep voice was firm, but there was guarded interest in his eyes.

Against her better judgment, she said, "I could give you a quick tour after our meal."

"Thank you. We gladly accept," Gwen piped up.

It didn't appear that her friend Rose was quite as eager as she was.

Ada was trying to decide how best to remedy the tension emanating from Rose, when they were interrupted by Lilith Carlisle. She made a scene by, rather loudly, pushing her plate of food away in disgust. She arose indignantly, and she stalked past several tables before halting next to theirs.

"Why, Luke darling," she began with sickening sweetness, "you have quite a harem assembled today."

"Don't start anything." He began to stand.

Ada restrained him gently. She perused Lilith. "Miss Carlisle, they were just telling me how entertaining you are," she said drolly. "As an actress, of course."

"I'm sure." Lilith's chin tilted higher.

"I'm Ada Marsh—"

"I know who you are," she said with contempt.

"Is there anything we can do for you?"

"No. I just thought I'd warn you about him." She motioned to Luke. "That one will break your heart."

"I'm sure my fiancé would have something to say about that." Ada reached for her spoon. "We wouldn't dream of detaining you any longer. Perhaps we will meet again," she said lightly.

"Perhaps we shall." Lilith gave her a disquieting smile. With a swirl of her skirts, she was gone.

Luke chuckled. "Miss Marsh, I don't remember ever seein' her leave a room that quickly. I believe I'd like to thank you."

"And how would you do that, Mr. Logan?"

"How about a piece of pie?" He had a roguish gleam in his eyes. "How does gooseberry sound?"

Gwen laughed, and Rose reluctantly smiled.

Ada pursed her lips. "I have a feeling I've missed something."

"Gwen and I have been regaling Miss Dennis with our childhood exploits." He crossed his arms and leaned back in his chair. "Let me tell you about a girl and a gooseberry pie. . . ."

Chapter Four

As Luke escorted Gwen, Rose, and Miss Marsh down Main Street toward the theater, he wondered what kind of mess he was getting himself into.

Miss Marsh was the most entrancing woman he had ever met. She was lovely and amusing. He felt at ease with and in awe of her at the same time. Which was why he was disturbed. She would be leaving town in a week. He would never see her again. To top it all off, she was engaged to be married. He needed to put all sentimental ideas aside. He would not fall for this woman. He couldn't.

When they arrived, Ada led them down an alley. They went through the rear entrance so they could see what it was like backstage. They made their way down a dimly lit corridor with many doors.

"I came over before lunch and claimed my dressing room. One of the advantages of being the leading lady is procuring the largest room." Ada smiled.

She paused at one of the doors and let them in. Two large trunks were in the small room, their contents spilling out. Brilliant costumes were being aired. At the dressing table with a mirror, a case of cosmetics was open.

Gwen fingered a gold beaded Renaissance-style gown. "Where did you find something like this?" she asked in awe.

"I made it," she admitted.

"It's just beautiful. I could never do this kind of work."

"That's an understatement." Luke leaned against the doorframe with his hands in his pants pockets. He spoke to Ada, "You should see the last shirt she mended for me." He shook his head. "I'm afraid to sneeze in it for fear of it comin' apart and embarrassin' me."

"Oh, you!" Gwen made a face at him.

"Are they always like this?" Ada asked Rose.

Rose dimpled when she looked at Luke. "I'm afraid so."

Sweet Rose. Why couldn't he feel the same way about her as he did this woman who was practically a stranger? He must be dull-witted.

He tore his gaze from the contrasting women and pulled his watch out of his pocket. After pretending to note the time, he snapped the case shut. "I'm afraid I'll need to head back home soon. Got chores to do," he explained, knowing that wasn't the exact truth of the situation.

"Of course," Ada said kindly. "Follow me."

He breathed in the soft scent of her as she passed by. He had to get out of there before it was too late. Maybe it already was.

At the end of the hallway, a short flight of stairs led to the stage. They made their way through a maze of discarded sets. They startled a pretty young woman and a man who were gazing at each other.

"Lisette, Paul, I'm showing my companions around. Round everyone up and tell them I'll be ready for rehearsal momentarily," Ada instructed.

Lisette nodded, and she glanced nervously over her shoulder toward the stage.

"We'll find everyone." Paul took Lisette's elbow, and they hurried away.

Ada led them on and then stopped abruptly. The voluminous burgundy velvet curtains were open, and at center stage a couple was locked in an embrace and kissing ardently.

Luke cleared his throat loudly.

Hugh Wellington was in no hurry to look up from his activities.

Ada's face went blank. "I see you decided to begin without me," she said coldly.

Wellington untangled himself from the woman, who appeared extremely uncomfortable. "Myra and I were running through some scenes." He tugged at the bottom of his vest and straightened his tie.

"We . . . didn't know . . . if you were coming," Myra stammered.

"Apparently," Ada said under her breath.

Luke could see her trying to compose herself. So, it *was* as bad as it looked. Her fiancé was pawing another woman. If only he felt he had the right, he'd smack that arrogant smile off of Wellington's face.

"I will see you out," she told them quietly. She twirled from Hugh with her head held high.

"We will wait to continue, darling, until your return." Hugh's clipped words sounded untroubled.

Ada's spine stiffened.

Luke glared at him and put his hand to Ada's back. He propelled her forward. "Thank you for inviting us over, Miss Marsh," he said, loud and clear. "I don't know how you actors do it." He heard a grunt of amusement from Hugh Wellington.

They emerged from the building in uneasy silence. Ada raised a hand to shield her eyes from the blinding sunlight.

"Miss Marsh . . ." Gwen began.

"There's no need for formalities now—just call me Ada." Her voice wavered.

Luke stepped forward. "If you need anything—" The words caught in his throat. "If you need anything, Gwen lives a couple of blocks away at Mrs. Brown's boardinghouse."

Ada nodded and rubbed her temples.

"Good-bye, Miss Ada," he said, not knowing if they should leave or not.

They were walking away before her distressed voice stopped them.

"Wait! Will I see all of you again?" she beseeched them.

His gut wrenched for her. "You can bet on it."

Ada made her way to her dressing room. She had to calm herself before she saw Hugh again. Did he think she was some kind of simpleton? They never kissed that passionately onstage.

She put her hands on the dressing table, bowing her head. She breathed deeply. Her whole world was full of charlatans. She had actually been afraid to let her new acquaintances go. They seemed to be the only kind, respectable people she knew.

"Darling?" Hugh inquired.

She whirled to face him. Her eyes were blazing.

"Why, it appears my love is jealous," he teased.

"Get out!" She pointed to the door. "I won't be made a fool."

"Now, Ada . . ."

"I mean it. I'll find some local off the street to play your part."

"Ada." He grasped her sternly by the upper arms. "We were only rehearsing."

She turned her face from his.

"Myra was too enthusiastic." He put a finger under her chin and made her look at him.

Young Myra was the newest cast member. The impulsive blond had only been with them a month. She was a promising talent, but she had a lot to learn.

"Are you telling me that it was all her?" she whispered.

"Yes. She apologized as soon as you left." His eyes seemed to plead with her.

"Why should I believe you?"

He brushed a stray hair from her temple.

"Hugh. I want an answer." Her anger began to melt. "I need an answer."

"You should believe me because I adore you. You are my own true heart."

She sighed. "If I ever see you in someone's arms again . . ."

"You won't." He covered her lips with his. Then he pulled away and smiled. "Now, that's settled. Let's postpone rehearsals for an hour or so. We need some amusement. Let's explore this fascinating hamlet."

"Oh, I don't know. There's so much to do."

"Let's, my love. It would be a lark." He kissed the back of her fingers.

She couldn't resist his charm. "For an hour only," she agreed.

As they went into the hallway, Paul was coming toward them. "We're all ready," he called out to them.

"Inform them they have an hour's respite until our return," Hugh said over his shoulder as they walked away, Ada's hand tucked into the crook of his arm.

They left Paul standing there with an odd expression on his face.

Chapter Five

Ada and Hugh strolled along Main Street. The temperature was mild, and a gentle breeze made their time together enjoyable. People nodded to them as they went by. They soon came to an intersection, and their hotel was in view to the north.

Hugh paused in front of the House of Lords saloon. "Let me see if I can purchase some fine wine from this choice establishment."

"We don't need any, do we?"

"I thought we could have a little wine and cheese for a picnic." He chucked her under the chin. He left her standing in the middle of the sidewalk.

She could see through the propped-open door into the crowded bar as he entered. A burly man leered at her. She turned her back on the tavern. Luke Logan was across the street, emerging from the bank.

"Miss Ada." Luke greeted her with a raised hand as he made his way through the traffic.

She acknowledged him and took a step his way.

"I thought you were rehearsin'—"

His words were cut off by shouts and a shattering noise behind her. Two brawling men burst from the bar and crashed into her. They knocked her from her feet and sent her soaring. She tumbled to the brick street, skirts flying. She landed hard on her hip and elbow. Her sleeve was ripped, her arm stung, and one ankle felt twisted.

"Ada!" Luke ran to her. He yanked down the hem of her skirts to cover her legs. He put a strong arm around her. "Are you hurt?"

"I—I'm not sure." She lifted her arm. Blood oozed from her elbow.

She began to stand, and he assisted her to her feet. She winced from the searing pain in her ankle.

He swung her up into his arms as if she were no burden at all. He strode to the Norwood and carried her in.

"Miss Marsh has been injured!" he roared to the stunned clerk behind the counter. "Go get Dr. Maxwell."

"I don't think I'm hurt badly," she told him quietly.

"We'll let the doctor decide that."

People scurried out of the elevator as he barged in. He held her against his broad chest. She rested her head on his sturdy shoulder.

He spoke softly under his breath. She raised her head and saw that his eyes were closed but his lips were still moving.

"I'm sorry. What did you say?" she asked.

He focused on her. His countenance was concerned but calm. He shrugged and shifted her easily in his arms. "I was praying for you."

"Oh, really . . . I . . ." She gulped.

She was speechless. No one had ever prayed for her before, much less a strapping farmer. She blinked in surprise.

The elevator opened, and she directed him to her room. He deposited her safely on the bed. He snatched the towel from the washstand and dunked it into the pitcher of water. The mattress sank as he sat next to her. He unbuttoned the cuff of her sleeve and rolled it up carefully.

"You don't need to do this," she protested.

"I want to."

He raised her arm and dabbed at the grime and blood. His brow was creased as he bent over her.

"Good. It's not scraped too badly."

She inspected it and smiled at him.

He ducked his head. "I'm sorry about all this."

"It wasn't your fault." She was surprised by his apology.

"I saw it happening, but I couldn't stop it."

"It was just an unfortunate accident." She squeezed his hand. "Besides, you were there to gallantly rescue me. I would wager that all those busybodies in the lobby are still standing there with their mouths wide open." She chuckled.

He gave her a lopsided grin. "I bet you're right."

Suddenly Hugh stormed in through the open doorway. "What is happening here?" he demanded.

Luke sprang from the bed with a guilty expression on his face.

"Some men from the saloon knocked me down. Mr. Logan was kind enough to assist me," she explained.

"I would have been along presently." He glowered at Luke.

"I wasn't about to leave the lady sprawled in the street with her skirts around her ears," he defended himself.

"Now that you've done your duty, you may leave."

"Excuse me." An elderly man spoke from behind Hugh.

"Dr. Maxwell. Thank you for comin'," Luke said. He motioned to her. "This is Miss Marsh. She's injured her ankle."

"Well, let me see how I can help you, young lady." Dr. Maxwell went to her and deposited his bag at the end of the bed. She slightly raised her skirts and carefully slipped off her black leather shoe.

Luke respectfully turned away, went to the window, and studied the street below as the doctor examined her ankle. It moved her that Luke cared enough for propriety to avert his attention from her stockinged foot. She couldn't remember the last time she had been treated with such courtesy by a man.

Hugh, in the meantime, placed the wine bottle onto the chest of drawers and eased himself into a cushioned chair. He stroked his mustache while idly perusing Luke's rigid form.

"Well, Miss Marsh, you have a seriously sprained ankle. Stay in bed, and keep it elevated for several days. Be careful on it for a week or two after that," Dr. Maxwell instructed.

"But we have rehearsals, and the play is Saturday." Alarm crept into her voice.

"I'm sorry, Miss Marsh. You'll need to do as I say. You might be able to perform by Saturday, but you need to be aware of any tenderness and not overdo it."

"Thank you, Doctor." She was relieved by his words. "Hugh will see you out and pay you for your time."

Hugh nodded and departed with the doctor.

Luke came to her. "I'd better get goin'."

She nodded and grasped his hand. "Thank you for everything, Luke."

"You're more than welcome, Ada."

"Will you bring Gwen and Rose to see me, since I'll be confined for a few days?"

"Of course." He grinned. "I'd be glad to."

He released her hand, went to the door, and disappeared after a quick glance over his shoulder.

Luke Logan was an original. She wished he could have stayed. She would like to get to know him better. She knew that having those thoughts was treading on dangerous ground, though. She was engaged to Hugh. She shouldn't have any interest in another man.

During the days that followed, Ada had plenty of time to reflect on her life. Most men saw actresses as little more than harlots. She would never forget the whistles or innuendoes she and her fellow actresses had had to endure in St. Louis as they walked to nearby restaurants. Or the incident that was seared in her mind the most—when a man old enough to be her father had hidden backstage after a performance and grabbed her and pinned her against a wall. She would never forget the smell of his hot, drunken breath or the lewd things he'd whispered into her ear. She shuddered to think what might have occurred if Paul hadn't startled him and then thrown him out.

That's why Luke Logan was such a wonder to her. She hadn't met many true gentlemen in her travels. It was refreshing to feel she didn't need to be defensive around him.

The primary gentleman in her life, Hugh, was as attentive as he could be during this time. His days were hectic, as he directed and rehearsed as leading man in his pet project. He would come to visit her in the evenings, bringing up a supper tray. They would discuss rehearsals and read their lines together. He always seemed reluctant to leave but insisted she needed her rest.

As Luke placed the walking stick he'd made for Ada into the buggy, he began to feel that it wasn't as good an idea as he'd first thought. He had spent many hours the last few days on it. He'd found a long, straight branch from one of the red oaks on his land. He'd cut it, stripped the bark off, sanded it, and stained it dark red—like the color of her hair—and varnished it.

He was pleased with his work, but he suddenly felt unsure of himself. Maybe it wouldn't be wise to give it to her. He ran his fingers down the satiny-smooth length of it. He wouldn't be a coward. He'd made it for her. He would give it to her.

When he arrived in town, he picked up Rose and Gwen. As he drove to the hotel, he was too preoccupied to listen to their chatter. He wondered how Ada was faring, if she was feeling better and if she would really be glad to see them.

He was able to park in front of the Norwood. The three of them got down from the buggy.

When he picked up the cane, Gwen asked, "Where did you get that?"

"I made it for Miss Ada," he commented.

"You did? Why on earth would you do something like that?"

His scowl stopped her from going any further. He noticed that Rose looked pale. This was just wonderful. He knew he should somehow tell Rose that he wasn't the one for her, but now he'd hurt her before he had the chance to explain himself.

He silently cursed his luck as they entered the lobby. Their eyes were immediately drawn to Hugh Wellington and Lilith Carlisle. She was hanging on his arm as they strolled toward the restaurant. She

was whispering into his ear, and he seemed capti-
vated by her.

"That rat," Gwen muttered.

"They're both vermin," he concluded. "Come on."

He ushered them ahead, but not before Lilith
spotted them. She gave them a victorious smile as
she sauntered away with Wellington.

Luke wanted to wring his neck—and shout for
joy. He wanted to tell Ada what they had seen, but he
wasn't sure if he should.

Chapter Six

A knock interrupted Ada from reading her lines. She put the play aside and hobbled to the door. She opened it and found her new friends waiting.

"I'm so glad to see all of you." She moved aside to let them in.

"Should you be up yet?" Gwen asked as she took a seat by the window.

Rose sat on the edge of the other cushioned chair by the chest of drawers. Luke closed the door.

"It's not bad unless I'm up for a long time."

"Well, Luke has something to help," Gwen piped up.

Ada turned to him. He gave her a stylish walking stick. He ran his fingers through his hair, almost self-consciously, before leaning casually against a wall.

"He made it for you," Gwen informed her.

"You did?"

He nodded.

"It's magnificently crafted." She admired it. "I will treasure it always. Whenever I see it, I will remember my three friends in Shawnee."

She used the cane as she limped back to the bed. She beamed at Luke when she settled onto the coverlet. She placed the walking stick beside her.

"Do you think you will be able to perform by Saturday?" Gwen asked.

"I should be able to. There isn't a great deal of walking. I'm going to see how I fare at the dress rehearsal tomorrow afternoon. I'll decide then."

Gwen nodded.

"It just occurred to me," Ada began, "would the three of you like to come to the dress rehearsal? You could see how things are run behind the scenes." Her gaze flitted from face to face. "Would you be able to attend?"

"I'd love to," Gwen accepted quickly.

"I should be able to come," Luke consented with a grin.

"I can't," Rose stated rather coldly.

Gwen appeared perplexed as she watched Rose.

Luke shuffled his feet and asked, "What time do we need to be there?"

"Before three."

Ada fingered the neck of her blue calico wrapper. Rose's reserved demeanor made her uncomfortable. She had the feeling she had overstepped some boundary.

"You have plans for tomorrow?" Ada asked her politely.

"Yes." Rose toyed with the white fabric gloves in her lap. "I'm to meet the organist at church to practice a new song," she said softly.

"She sings like an angel," Gwen boasted.

"And plays the piano just as well," Luke said with admiration.

"That's quite a gift," Ada said with sincerity. "My voice is marginal, at best."

Rose seemed to squirm at being the center of attention, but a small smile appeared. "It's difficult to believe that someone as accomplished as you would have any shortcomings." Her words were cautious but genuine.

"Not only can't I sing, I can't cook, either." She made fun of herself. "My grandmother used to tell me that the way to a man's heart was through his stomach. I learned quickly that I'd have to distract them enough with prose and dance until they forgot they were ever hungry," she confided to Rose.

A lilting giggle erupted from her, and she eased back into her chair. "It can't be that terrible."

"Well, let's see...." Ada tapped her forehead. "The last time I cooked for my grandmother, I burned the toast and scorched the oatmeal, and the scrambled eggs would have bounced all the way to Arkansas," she told them with a wry smile. "Needless to say, she encouraged me to learn to sew. Then I could become a seamstress and hire a cook someday."

Everyone laughed. Ada felt she had finally befriended Rose. For some reason it was meaningful that such a gentle soul as Rose should approve of her. Maybe it was because she wished to have peace in her own life. She was more determined than ever to tell Hugh her desires. She would talk to him as soon as possible.

They had visited a good hour before Gwen reminded Luke that she had an article to write. As they were leaving, he wanted to tell Ada that he had seen Lilith with Hugh Wellington, but he couldn't. He just couldn't stand the thought of seeing her radiant expression crumble. Still, he felt he should have warned her.

He dropped Gwen off and drove Rose home. He pulled Samson to a stop at the end of the walkway. He hopped down and held a hand up to her. Her smile was nervous as she clasped his hand. He assisted her to the ground. She fidgeted with a lace cuff of her white shirtwaist.

"I'll walk you to the door, if you'd like," Luke offered. He had to explain things to her. Now was the time.

"Yes, please," she agreed.

They ambled up the walk. Yellow roses were beginning to bloom in front of the porch. He climbed the steps with her.

"Would you like to join me?" She motioned to the porch swing.

"Go ahead."

He removed his hat while she arranged herself in the swing. He sat near her on the white porch railing, one boot hanging in the air.

"I . . . uh . . . needed to talk to you." He fiddled with the brim of his hat.

"Yes?"

Her face was surprisingly blank. He could usually read her pretty easily. Not this time. He just had to forge on.

"I wanted to apologize if I . . . or Gwen . . . misled you. What I mean to say is that you're a wonderful young woman, and I'm tickled that we've become friends—"

She held a hand up. "You don't need to say any more."

"I just didn't want you to think—"

"I understand. Truly." She swallowed hard. "When are you going to tell her you're interested in her?"

"Her? You mean Ada?" He stared at a scuff mark on the toe of his boot. "She'll be leavin' in a few days. Besides, she's engaged."

"Well, I know I couldn't compete with her whether she's here or not," Rose said quietly.

"Rose, it's not you." He studied her.

She looked past him and remained silent.

"Rose, listen to me," he said plopping his hat onto the rail. "You're a sweet, talented person."

She smirked.

"It's me. I'm not good enough for you." He got to his feet and paced in front of her. "You deserve a man who's not distracted, someone who can cherish you, who sees only you," he tried to explain.

"Don't vex yourself, Luke." Her voice quavered. She took a deep breath and said, "I realized this afternoon that we weren't meant for each other."

He squatted in front of her. "Really?"

She nodded. "I was jealous, which isn't like me. But . . . she's captivating. I can't help but like her too."

"I was hoping you wouldn't be angry with me."

She put a tentative hand on his arm. "I hope someday a man will look at me the way you do her."

He bowed his head, took her hand, and pressed his lips to it. He peered up at her. "I know it'll happen."

She gave him a gentle smile.

"Thank you for understandin'." He stood and moved toward the stairs.

"Luke, you should talk to her."

He raised his palms. "How can I?"

"She needs to know what kind of man she's engaged to."

"Maybe she already knows. Maybe that's how those actors are." He shrugged. "We don't know her that well. She might have men on the side too."

"You don't really believe that, do you?" she asked sharply.

He shook his head.

"You saw how crushed she was when we saw him kissing that girl. She needs to know."

"How do you tell someone that her future husband is an immoral fool?"

"You'll find a way," she assured him.

"That's easier said than done." He retrieved his hat and jammed it onto his head. "But you're right."

"Of course I am." Spirit filled her voice. She waved him away. "Now, go on before it's too late."

"I will." He put a hand over his heart. "Thank you, Rose."

"You're welcome, Luke."

He bounded down the steps and saluted her before he climbed into the buggy. He snapped the reins. Whether it was wise or not, he was off to speak to Ada. If only he knew what to say.

Chapter Seven

Time was approaching for Hugh to return for their evening meal. Ada decided to surprise him and meet him downstairs.

She took time with her toilet. She rearranged her hair, spritzed herself with her favorite cologne, and changed her clothes. She put on a new dress that she had just completed. It was made of airy white lawn with delicate Irish lace at the collar and on the cuffs of the half sleeves. Sheer lace had been inserted horizontally along the hem. It had taken her many hours to embroider tiny white flowers over the entire dress.

She appraised herself in the full-length mirror. She had done a fine job. She knew Hugh would be impressed.

She picked up her cane and limped down the hall to the elevator. There was still a twinge of pain in her ankle, but it was bearable. As she emerged from the elevator, she remembered a small secluded alcove nearby. She decided to sit there and wait for Hugh. She would be able to see both the stairs and elevator from that vantage point.

Before she turned the corner, she heard some muffled voices and a giggle from that area. She was deciding whether to intrude when she caught sight of the couple.

Hugh was settled on the sofa with his hands in a woman's black hair. His lips were lingering on the other woman's as Ada's cane clattered to the floor.

Hugh jumped up and was struggling to compose himself. Lilith Carlisle stared at her boldly and lounged with an elbow on the back of the couch.

Ada caught her breath with a convulsive intake of air. She covered her mouth with a shaking hand. Blood rushed in her ears.

"It is not what it appears. . . ." Hugh started.

"Not what it appears?" She gulped, trying to suppress the bile threatening to rise. "What else could it be?"

He attempted an explanation. "We were—"

"I don't know who is the bigger fool, you or I,"

she interrupted. But blackness was beginning to engulf her.

"Miss Ada?" Luke's voice was behind her. "Are you ill?"

"Good-bye." She choked on the word she spoke to Hugh.

She stepped back, her ankle gave way, and she stumbled. Luke's long strides crossed the boards swiftly. He seized her before she could fall. He glanced at the scene and seemed to guess what was happening.

"Take me away from here," she whispered to Luke.

"After I take care of this—" He moved forward with his free fist clenched.

"Now." Her voice was strained. "Please . . ."

Her knees began to buckle. Luke quickly supported her by one elbow. He gave Hugh an icy glare before he led her away.

They hurried out of the hotel without looking back. He lifted her into his buggy and tucked her skirts around her legs.

Luke's tender care of her was too much. Ada buried her face in her hands and sobbed. She could not believe what Hugh had done. His disrespectful, hypocritical wantonness pierced her heart. Never again would she allow herself to fall under a man's spell. Never.

Luke stopped Samson in a shady, secluded spot in Woodland Park. He had never felt as helpless as he did now, watching Ada weep. He ached to take her into his arms to comfort her.

He dug a large red bandana out of his back pocket. Thankfully, it was clean.

"Ada?" He held it out to her.

She seemed to move in slow motion as she took it from him. She dabbed away her tears and wiped her nose. She took several deep, shuddering breaths.

"Thank you," she said. She found a dry edge of the handkerchief and blotted her eyes. "It seems you are forever coming to my rescue."

"I'm just in the right places at the right times."

He watched her struggle to gain her composure. The dappled sunlight caressed her. Her filmy blouse fluttered in the gentle breeze. Her dark eyelashes were damp, and the tip of her little nose was red, but he still thought she'd never looked more beautiful.

A tear slid down her cheek. "Why did this happen to me?"

"We're only human. We choose our own paths. Sometimes we make a mess of it."

Her spine stiffened. Just when he thought she was going to argue with him, she slumped into the cushion. She laid her head back and seemed to examine the green leaves overhead.

"I definitely made a mess." She sighed. "I didn't even like Hugh when I first met him."

"Is that so?"

"Yes. I thought he was an egotistical dandy. He was a good actor, though, so I hired him. He soon charmed me, and I forgave his faults. But not this time."

He cleared his throat. "So, there won't be a reconciliation?"

"No." Her voice didn't waver.

His heart pounded a little harder. He reached out to touch her arm.

"I'll never trust him—or any other man—again."

He snatched his hand back and adjusted the fit of his hat. "Surely you don't mean that."

"Of course I do. Men are lechers who cannot control themselves. I've seen it time and time again," she spat out.

"We're not all like that," he said gruffly.

She sat up and eyed him suspiciously. "Oh, no?"

"I'm not," he stated firmly. He stared back at her.

"So, when you reached for me just now, there was

no fleshly intent on your part?" She crossed her arms.

He was taken aback by her coarseness.

"I see you're at a loss for words, Mr. Logan," she said with a haughty tilt to her chin.

"I was only stunned by your crudeness, Miss Marsh." He loomed over her, squinting at her. "*I* am not like those other men," he ground out.

"So you say." She pursed her lips.

He wanted to throttle her. He closed and opened his hands, scanning the creases in his calloused palms. He inhaled deeply. "I am a simple man. I've worked hard. I'm also a man of my word," he said softly. "And when I tell you the truth, I expect you to believe it."

She continued to watch him.

"I believe in the sacredness of the marriage bed." He was blunt, as she had been. "And I'm not goin' to share it with anyone other than my wife."

Her jaw dropped.

"I'm not goin' to lie and say I'm not attracted to you. But I would never do anything to be ashamed of. And I sure wouldn't make any kind of advances if you didn't want me to."

He picked up the reins. "I only wanted to comfort you," he stated as he snapped the leather.

He pulled into the traffic on Broadway. Ada remained silent all the way to Mrs. Brown's boardinghouse. He guessed he had given her something to chew on.

When they arrived, he escorted her to Gwen's room. He told Gwen as much as he thought prudent about the situation. She didn't disappoint him, generously offering to share her room with Ada.

As soon as that was settled, he left for home. The sun was low on the horizon. He would make it home just before dark.

He wagged his head as he remembered the events of the day. The women in his life were brave, funny, kind, and fiery. He was going to have to stay on his toes to keep up with them. They seemed to be more trouble than they were worth. Well, almost.

Chapter Eight

Early the next morning, Ada and Gwen caught a ride with the milk deliveryman to the Norwood to gather her things. She knew her fellow actors would still be sound asleep. She didn't want to face any of them yet. Rehearsal that afternoon would be soon enough.

Gwen helped her pack her valise and trunk. They searched out the hotel coach driver, and Ada paid him handsomely to carry them to the boarding-house. Gwen tried to assure her that Luke would do it for her, but she just couldn't bother him.

She had treated him badly, and he'd still shared intimate details about himself. She felt foolish. She shouldn't have goaded him the way she did. She should not have assumed he was like every other man she had known. There was a comforting calmness about him. She had sensed it from that first luncheon, but she hadn't admitted it to herself. She wasn't planning to get close to any man, but she wouldn't put them all in the same category now. She would remember his sincerity when she left with the troupe in a few days.

The fleeting thought of her acting company made her uneasy. She had always suffered from mild nerves before going onstage, but now she felt ill thinking about performing. She would just have to ignore the queasiness and do it.

That afternoon, the time neared for Gwen and Rose and Luke to go to the theater with Ada, but Luke had not arrived. Gwen surmised that something on the farm must have kept him away. Ada, on the other hand, couldn't help but think she had made him angry.

They had been waiting on a bench by the front steps, and finally Gwen got up and dashed around the side of the house. She returned shortly, pushing a two-seated bicycle.

"I hate to see you walk all that way. So, here's our solution." She grinned.

Ada raised her eyebrows. "Where did you get that?"

"Mrs. Brown lets us use it when we need to."

"Well . . ."

"Rose and I have ridden it several times. It's perfectly safe."

"Is it more difficult than a standard bicycle?" She knew she sounded skeptical.

"Not much. I'll be in front. You just follow me," Gwen joked.

Ada chuckled. "Let's give it a try."

After a rather shaky start, they were off. They arrived with all body parts intact. The momentary thrill of the ride vanished when they leaned the bicycle against the back of the theater. A sense of dread washed over Ada. Her palms were sweaty as she removed her gloves and put them into her handbag. Her heart thudded painfully.

"I can't do this," she whispered. She backed against the building and bent forward, her hands on her knees.

"What's wrong?" Gwen put an arm over her shoulders.

She swallowed hard. "The thought of being on-stage . . . with him . . . makes me sick."

"Don't do it, then. You have an understudy. She can do it until you feel better," Gwen reasoned.

Ada nodded, but she knew by the way her legs were trembling that it would be a long time before she could perform again.

"I'll help you tell them, if you need me," Gwen encouraged as she helped her up.

"Good."

Ada felt her condition was dubious, but she led the way to her dressing room. Through the open door, a costumed Myra was visible. She sat at the dressing table, patting her face with powder.

"Oh, Ada." She put a hand to her chest. "You startled me."

"Why are you wearing my gown?" she inquired, none too politely.

"Well . . . um . . ." Myra stammered. She looked like a frightened rabbit. "Hugh said your injury would prevent you from performing."

"He did, did he? Where is he?" Anger was beginning to overtake her, and that wasn't good. She tended to do rash things when her ire was up.

"In his dressing room . . . I think."

Ada charged down the hall, forgetting about her tender ankle. Gwen followed closely on her heels. Ada flung Hugh's door open and stood in the entryway, hands on hips.

He seemed cool and calm as he placed his comb on his dressing table. He swiveled on his stool and lounged back with his elbows on the table.

"Ah, my dear Ada, we assumed you wouldn't make an appearance today," he began.

"You presumptuous, arrogant—" she sputtered.

"Now, now. Anger doesn't suit you at all." He smirked and waved her away. "If you wish, tell Myra to disrobe. Then you may join me onstage."

"Join you? I'll never join you in any capacity again."

He stroked his mustache. "It will be rather awkward, don't you think? The two sweethearts of the troupe never to be seen onstage together? Doesn't appear to be a sound decision to me."

"I take it you think you know how to run this company as well as I do?" She narrowed her eyes at him. The nerve of him. She had hired him. She could fire him—right now. Yet she was so tired of traveling. Tired of it all. She felt her life altering at that very moment.

He remained silent. His eyebrows rose with a pompous air.

"Firing you is my first instinct, but I've decided I want a change. If you can come up with the funds before you leave town, you can buy me out. Otherwise, the Ada Marsh Players are no more."

She could see concern for his livelihood flit across his face before he spoke. "I'll buy this little production. The Hugh Wellington Revue has a nice ring to it, does it not?"

"See how far you get without me," she said with

contempt. "I will find an attorney, settle on a price, and sign over my rights. I'll have the lawyer bring you the paperwork. I'm out."

For the first time since she had known him, Hugh was speechless.

She turned from him for the last time. She grabbed Gwen, who stood transfixed, by the arm, and she limped away with her head held high.

They were soon outside in the bright sunshine. With a worried glance backward, Gwen asked, "Oh, Ada, are you sure you want to do this?"

"Yes." She nodded as she accepted what she had just done. "I'm more than a gypsy. I want a home. I'm ready to move on with my life. Hugh helped me realize rather quickly and painfully what kind of life I do want for myself."

"Where are you going to live?"

That decision was easy to make. "I would like to live here, in Shawnee."

"How wonderful!" Gwen grasped her hands. "There'll be a vacancy at Mrs. Brown's at the end of the month. One of the girls living there is getting married."

"Perfect. It seems to be a quiet, respectable establishment." She scrunched up her face in thought. "I'll have some money, but I will want an income. I don't suppose this town needs a seamstress."

"You're not going to believe this," Gwen gushed. "Mrs. Parkinson, who owns a little dressmaker's shop, was just in the newspaper office to place an ad for help."

"No!"

"Yes. Let's go. It's only a couple of blocks over on Bell Street."

"Do I look presentable enough for an interview?" She glanced down at her pink lawn shirtwaist and brown walking skirt.

"You look beautiful, as always." Gwen pulled her along. "Let's go!"

The shop was one of several small businesses at street level in the two-story redbrick building. An elegant gown and a practical dress were displayed in the large plate-glass window. A bell jingled over the door as Ada and Gwen entered.

Tall shelves laden with bolts of colorful fabrics lined each side of the long, narrow room. One table toward the front was covered with tidy bolts of calicos and other inexpensive materials. Another oak table was bare except for a yardstick and a pair of scissors.

Two doors were in the back wall. The one at the far left corner had mirrors nearby. Presumably, that was the fitting room. The other door had to lead to the workroom, for a thin, middle-aged woman emerged from it.

She was attired professionally and sensibly. A measuring tape was draped around her neck. She wore a navy blue tie over a crisp white shirtwaist with starched cuffs and collar. Her navy wool skirt skimmed the shiny oak floors. Her graying brown hair was pulled back into a severe bun. Wire-rimmed eyeglasses perched on her hawk nose.

"Miss Sanders, how may I assist you?" Mrs. Parkinson looked over her glasses at them. She seemed friendly enough.

"Mrs. Parkinson, this is Ada Marsh."

"The actress?" She squinted at her.

"Yes, ma'am. She recently decided to retire from the theatrical profession." After no response, Gwen forged on. "I told her that you were seeking an assistant."

"You can sew?" She pursed her thin lips.

"Quite well," Ada responded.

"She does magnificent work. I've seen it," Gwen offered.

"Did you happen to bring an example?"

Ada glanced at her empty hands and raised her arms. "I made this waist."

Mrs. Parkinson inspected the fine stitching and the small tucks on the yoke. She fingered the cuffs and seemed to note the tiny brown flowers embroidered at the wrists and neck.

"The embroidery?"

"I did that also."

The proprietor stood back and eyed her up and down. "This is a respectable establishment, Miss Marsh. I would expect decorum at all times. In and out of the shop."

Ada drew herself up. "I never conduct myself in any other way."

Mrs. Parkinson nodded thoughtfully. "I could pay you a dollar a day."

"That's acceptable."

"Can you begin Monday morning?"

"Yes."

"Fine. Be here promptly at eight." Mrs. Parkinson extended her hand. "Welcome, Miss Marsh."

"Thank you." Ada shook her hand and made her exit.

Relief flooded over her as they left the shop. When they were out of sight, she hugged her new friend.

"You've been such a help, Gwen."

"I'm happy to do it." She draped an arm over Ada's shoulders. "Now, let's go talk to Mrs. Brown and find you a home."

"Yes. Let's."

Chapter Nine

As Luke rode his skittish sorrel mare, Daisy, along the fence line, thoughts of Ada crowded back into his mind. He'd had a hard time all week concentrating on his work. He had hoped riding his new horse out to mend fences would calm them both, but it hadn't worked yet.

He knew Ada was long gone, but he could envision her as if she were standing right in front of him. She was amazing. He didn't know how to get her out of his mind, but he knew he needed to.

He had been almost relieved the previous Friday when he couldn't make it to the dress rehearsal. He couldn't have made Samson pull a buggy when he was favoring a foreleg. He could have tried to take Daisy to town, but he didn't trust her in a crowd. He knew, for his own sanity, it was best not to see Ada again anyway. So he hid out at his farm and tried to make some sense of things.

He sorted through his feelings for that redheaded actress and finally came to the realization that anything he felt for her was hopeless. She had a life of her own out there. It would be stupid to pine for such a complicated woman. Still, it had been mighty hard not to go into town and try to stop her from getting on that train.

She had been gone almost a week now. He would try to resume his simple, uncomplicated life. And— he shook his head—his lonely life. It would be a long time before he would forget her. He wasn't sure he ever could.

Ada closed up the shop on Saturday. She was straightening bolts of cloth on the table when she realized how the week had flown by. She had been busy enough to keep from mourning the loss of her friends, who left on Monday.

Paul, Lisette, and Sara had found her at the boardinghouse on Sunday. They brought her a trunk of her personal costumes and said their farewells.

They seemed stunned by her withdrawal from the troupe and said they were sorry she wouldn't be with them anymore. She would miss them too.

If she was honest with herself, she did feel a twinge of apprehension when she heard the train blow its departing whistle Monday. Her old life was leaving with that train. She hoped she'd made the right decision to stay in Shawnee.

The week had been encouraging, though. Despite being the object of curious and even bold stares in the beginning, it seemed the women who frequented the dress shop were accepting her. She felt they trusted her suggestions about style, choice of fabrics, and colors. She was beginning to gain confidence in her new profession. She was gratified at the end of each day.

Gwen had been a gracious hostess and was becoming a trusted friend. She would almost be sad when she moved to her own room in a few days. Their shared evenings, getting acquainted, had been fun. Ada liked her better and better the more she got to know her. Gwen was genuine, creative, and spunky. And she cared for everyone. Luke, especially, was like one of her brothers.

Luke. Now, that was a complicated subject. With Hugh out of her life and hundreds of miles away, her thoughts lingered on the farmer. He was a most fascinating specimen. She knew she was bound to see him often. She hoped she hadn't offended him so much that they couldn't all be friends. Friendship was the only thing she wanted from him. She wasn't going to fall for any man again. Not even him.

Sunday morning dawned cool with cloudless blue skies. Ada was up early and sat by the window to see the sunrise. She hoped it would calm her after a restless night. She was going to church with Gwen. It had seemed like a reasonable way to start her new life when she agreed to go, but now she wasn't so sure.

She hadn't set foot in a church since her grandmother's funeral. It had not been a conscious decision at the time. She just fell into a style of life where going to services was difficult to accomplish.

Was she being a hypocrite to go after all these years? Was she just trying to act the proper lady and do what was expected? She wasn't sure if she should go, but she felt compelled to do so.

Luke stopped his buggy near St. Benedict's Church at Ninth and Park Streets. The modest white clapboard church sat on a corner lot. The new church they were going to build over on Kickapoo would be grand compared to this one.

Someone was ringing the bell in the small bell tower at the crest of the roof above the double doors. He bounded up the wide gray steps and let himself into the tiny vestibule. He paused to remove his hat and run his fingers through his hair. He straightened his bow tie as he scanned the congregation for Gwen and Rose.

The white walls reflected the light from the rows of windows on both sides of the church. Aisles ran the length of the building down the center and along the walls. A row of oak pews lined either side of the middle aisle. Large curtains were pulled aside, exposing the altar. The church was also used as a school during the week, and the altar area was closed off at those times.

He spotted Rose with her parents in the back row, in front of the organ. It took several moments before he recognized Gwen's straw hat. She was sitting toward the front.

There seemed to be a buzz in the air as he and a few stragglers made their way to their seats. His boot heels echoed on the wood floor as he strode over to Gwen.

Gwen acknowledged him with a big smile and slid over toward the middle of the pew. The woman who was at the end didn't see him from around the brim of her enormous black hat, so he stepped past her to sit next to his cousin. It was only then that the woman looked up. He almost stumbled when Ada lifted her face toward him.

He sat down heavily before he embarrassed himself. His pulse quickened. He'd never thought he would see Ada again, yet here she was. And she was a sight to behold. She wore a dark green suit trimmed with black. The color of her outfit made her emerald eyes even more captivating.

He inserted the brim of his hat into a clip on the back of the pew in front of him. He grinned at Gwen and turned to Ada with questions written all over his face.

She gave him a tentative smile and an expression that promised answers later.

The congregation stood. Luke plucked a hymnal from the holder in front of Ada. He flipped to the correct page, held it up for her, and sang along with his fellow worshipers. He wasn't a great singer, but he always gave it his best. He didn't know why Ada had said she couldn't carry a tune, because she was a fine singer.

During the service, Luke had a difficult time concentrating as young Reverend Schneider read the gospel. Being so near Ada was distracting.

When the service was ending, they stood for the final hymn. Rose's pure soprano voice enveloped the congregation as she led the singing.

The hairs prickled on the back of Luke's neck as he listened to Rose. He always loved to hear her sing. He glanced down at Ada. She appeared surprised and touched by Rose's abilities. She placed a gloved hand over her heart.

Ada exited the church, tilting her head so the brim of her hat would block the bright sun. She nodded to the exuberant minister. His brown hair was parted down the middle. His gray eyes studied her through the wire spectacles on his thin nose.

"Miss Marsh," he greeted her. "Some of the parishioners told me you were joining us today. Welcome." His teeth were crooked, but his smile was genuine.

"I enjoyed your sermon. It was illuminating," she told him sincerely.

He bent his head to her in thanks before turning to the man behind her.

She proceeded down the steps and moved away from the inquisitive looks from various members of the congregation. She was accustomed to putting on a façade of confidence. It would take time to relax and be herself among the strangers here.

She recognized Luke's horse and surrey. She wandered over to it. She removed a black glove and held her hand under the gelding's mouth. His velvety nose sniffed her palm. The bridle jingled as he tossed his head. He snorted and nuzzled her hand. She stroked the white star on his forehead.

"Samson doesn't like just anyone," Luke said softly from behind her.

"I'm honored to be so admired, Samson." She gave him a final pat before turning to Luke.

"I was surprised to see you this mornin'," he commented.

"Surprised to see me in church or in Shawnee?" she teased.

"Both." He gave her a lopsided grin. "Did you and the other actors decide to stay in town a while?"

"No. I. . . ." She began uncertainly. "I was tired of that life. They went on without me. I'm going to make a new start here."

His guarded eyes lit up.

She averted her gaze. She wasn't ready for the fondness she could read in his brown eyes. It frightened her.

She was glad to be interrupted by Gwen and Rose, who came up to them. She met them with outstretched arms.

"Rose, you sang wonderfully." She hugged her

and gave her a quick peck on the cheek. "I was so moved."

"That's so kind of you." Rose blushed. She turned the conversation away from herself by asking, "What are the three of you going to do today?"

Gwen shrugged. Luke shuffled his feet.

Rose caught Luke's eye. "Have you taken Ada out to your place yet?"

"No." He raised his eyebrows as he faced Ada.

"Yes!" Gwen exclaimed. "It's a beautiful day. We could have a picnic."

"Sounds good to me. How about it, Ada?" Luke asked.

"It does sound nice," she agreed. She turned to Rose. "You'll be joining us, won't you?"

"Oh, no. My parents invited some acquaintances and their eligible son for luncheon. I wouldn't want to miss that," she said in good cheer. "I'd better run. Mother and I need to go home and finish cooking." She backed away and waved. "Have a delightful day."

"Well, Mr. Bachelor, do you have anything edible out at your house?" Gwen inquired, knuckles on her hips.

"As a matter of fact, I do. Yesterday Mrs. Engel, my kindly neighbor, made her husband bring over an extra loaf of bread, some cooked ham, and even an apple pie."

"She must think you're getting too thin." Gwen hugged his slender waist and patted his solid stomach.

"Naw, she just misses her son since he moved to Oklahoma City." He squeezed her shoulders. "Now, let's get goin'. All this talk of food is makin' me hungry."

He moved away from Gwen and bowed to Ada with a gleam in his eye. "Miss Marsh, you are cordially invited to a picnic at the Logan farm. Fine food and entertainment will be provided. Are you interested?"

"Who wouldn't be?"

Chapter Ten

Ada relished the ride into the countryside. She filled her lungs with fresh air as she watched the passing rural landscape. Before long, homes were fewer and farther between.

She caught her breath when they turned off the road. Young oak saplings lined the long driveway to Luke's house. Rolling fields of green crops flanked the drive. His home was nestled amid tall trees. It looked like the perfect peaceful retreat.

A whitewashed fence encompassed a large front yard. A porch centered the front of the highly pitched–roofed house. A windmill stood between the house and barn. The blades turned slowly in the gentle breeze.

Luke stopped Samson in the shade of a cedar tree next to the expansive rear porch. The rails were painted white, the steps and planks were dark green, and the ceiling was sky blue. Two rocking chairs awaited occupants to view the wooded area behind the house.

He opened the squeaky screen door and led them into the kitchen past the solid white door. He plucked a shirt off a chair next to the table that was positioned near the door under a window.

"You'll have to excuse the mess, ladies. I wasn't expectin' company." With the toe of one boot, he nudged his dusty work boots out of the way under the table.

"Oh, please. You're tidier than an old maid." Gwen waved him aside. "Let me show Ada around."

Ada smiled at him as he rolled his eyes at his cousin.

Two doors led from the small kitchen. One, to the right, went into a hallway. The one straight ahead opened into the front parlor. Gwen escorted Ada into the simply furnished living area.

A black wood-burning stove stood against one wall. A long green tapestry sofa with upholstered arms sat under a bare window. A matching upholstered rocker with sturdy golden oak arms was placed nearby. A small table and a coatrack by

the front door were the remainder of the furnish-
ings.

The small foyer led into a short hallway. They
passed one tidy bedroom with a bed and a dresser. A
small bathroom was situated between that room and
the next. The other bedroom was Luke's. A white
wrought-iron bed was pushed against a wall. The
jacket and hat he had been wearing lay on the rumpled white and blue honeycomb bedspread. A metal
washstand with pitcher, bowl, and mirror was next to
the bed in front of a window. A towel with a blue
stripe hung from the stand. There was even a holder
for his shaving mug and razor. Under the other window, a small desk with stacks of papers on it faced
out into the backyard.

Ada felt uncomfortable invading Luke's personal
space, so she did not stay long. As she turned to
leave, she noticed that a drawer in the bureau was
slightly open, and a sock was hanging out. She resis-
ted the urge to put it back into its place.

They stepped across the hall and back into the
kitchen. They found Luke slicing bread at the
counter. Black suspenders molded to his strong
shoulders. Muscles brought on from hard work
shifted under his white shirt. His collar was unbuttoned, and his sleeves were rolled up. He was a man
at ease with himself.

He raised his head when they entered.

"You have a lovely home, Luke."

"I'm proud of it." He grinned. "It probably needs a woman's touch, though. Curtains, frilly things, and such."

"I would have offered to help but . . ." Gwen began as she removed her jacket and placed it on the back of a chair.

"But we know all too well about your sewing skills," he said.

"Oh, you." She took the knife from him and prodded him out of the way. "Go make yourself useful, and let us get lunch ready."

"Yes, ma'am," he responded, winking at Ada as he sauntered out of the room.

Luke left Gwen and Ada in his kitchen. Ada Marsh was in his house. If someone had predicted that two weeks ago, he would have told him to get out of the sun. Here she was, though, and his heart ached to know her better. Now he had the chance. She was staying in Shawnee. He wouldn't let her go this time. He knew he would have to bide his time before he could come forward with his tender feelings for her, but he was a patient man. He was more than willing to wait for Ada.

He went into the extra bedroom and opened a

drawer in the dresser. He found the log-cabin quilt his mother had made for him before he moved to Shawnee. He tucked it under his arm. His boots thumped across the pine floors as he returned to the kitchen.

Gwen informed him they were just about ready, so he leaned against the doorjamb to watch. Ada had removed her jacket also. She was searching through the cabinets. She gave a triumphant yelp when she located the green enameled plates and cups. She brought down three of each and spun around. She caught him spying on her. He would swear he saw her blush before she went to help Gwen and was hidden from his view.

Gwen covered the food with red-and-white–checkered napkins. She handed him the plate of sandwiches. She carried the pie, and Ada had the dishes and utensils.

They headed outside and walked into the wooded area behind the house. He led them to a small natural outcropping of large red sandstone rocks. He spread the quilt out underneath an enormous pecan tree.

Gwen put the pie plate down and exclaimed, "I forgot the drinks. Was that apple cider I saw in your icebox?"

He nodded.

"Good. I'll be right back." She dashed away.

He and Ada knelt to deposit their items on the quilt. He was reaching for the plates, when Ada gently touched his sleeve. He met her gaze.

"Luke, I'm glad we have a moment alone."

He was more than curious for her to continue.

"I need to apologize for the way I treated you last week. I feel terrible about it." Her eyes were pained.

He covered her hand with his. "You'd just had the shock of a lifetime."

"I know, but I shouldn't have made such assumptions about you."

"Apology accepted." He patted her hand. "Forget all about it."

She gave him an endearing smile. One that was meant only for him. His innards quaked. She probably wouldn't be too impressed with his moral views if she knew how much he hoped to kiss her someday.

Gwen crashed through the timber with a crockery pitcher held high.

Luke and Ada moved apart. He put his fingers to his forehead. "Now, that vision brings back painful memories."

Gwen stopped in her tracks and scowled at him. "How many times do I have to tell you that was an accident?" she huffed, plopping down next to them. "Besides, it was all Peter's fault."

"Why do I have the feeling there's some bad blood between you two?" Ada asked playfully.

"There is," he said with a haughty incline to his chin. "Let's see, I believe it was the summer after I graduated from school." He rubbed the vertical scar above his right eyebrow. "Our families had just moved to Guthrie. I had been living and working at a local ranch, and I came home for a weekend. I began to take notice of this sweet new neighbor named Enid."

"Little did he know, his older brother, Peter, had noticed her months earlier," Gwen told Ada behind her hand.

"As I was sayin', I charmed Enid to let me sit with her on her front porch. We were havin' polite conversation when—"

"More like you were making cow eyes at her," Gwen teased.

He struggled to keep a straight face. "I have never regarded any young woman with the orbs of a bovine."

His companions tittered.

"Anyway, Enid and I were conversing, when Gwen comes tearin' up the steps with a huge pitcher of water, screamin' like a banshee."

Ada raised her lovely eyebrows.

"Now, let me explain myself," Gwen interrupted. "Peter did not appreciate the goings-on over there, so he paid me to throw a pitcher of water at Luke to cool him off. If it made Luke look foolish in the process, Peter would have been even more pleased."

"And how much was this sabotage worth to him?" Ada inquired.

"A shiny nickel." Gwen's eyes gleamed.

"So, how did this result in your . . . unfortunate injury?" Ada tilted her face to him.

"Well, Miss Financier came runnin' up the stairs, and she tripped on the last tread."

"I've always been graceful," Gwen mused aloud.

"I tried to dodge her, but, instead, I stumbled forward as she was tryin' to catch herself with the pitcher. My forehead unhappily met with the item at hand." He rubbed the spot in question. "The next thing I remember is wakin' up with several stitches and the makings of a real beauty of a black eye."

"Oh, my." Ada covered a smile with her hand. "What happened with the enchanting Enid?"

He cleared his throat. "Apparently, my reluctance to protect her, along with my blood on her new skirt, didn't endear me to her. She married Peter that winter."

Ada laughed. "Don't give up on love, Luke. Your luck is bound to change."

Their eyes locked. The warmth he saw there encouraged him. "I believe my fortune has turned recently. And I won't be givin' up this time."

Chapter Eleven

Ada was rejuvenated by her trip to Luke's farm. It was a lovely spot. The day would have been perfect except for his obvious attraction to her. She had to admit she was flattered. That still didn't change the fact that she had already made up her mind not to trust men, so she would have to be strong in her resolve. If he persisted for long, she would need to set him straight before he became attached.

A few days later, she moved into her new home. Gwen helped her make quick work of relocating her things to the room behind Gwen's. Ada sewed a curtain of creamy brocade and hung it over the solitary window that looked out over the small backyard. A serviceable burgundy quilted comforter covered the simple wooden bed that was pushed against the wall to the left of the door. There was a chest of drawers and a tiny washstand with a cracked bowl. Two rickety chairs and a little round table were placed by the window. A blue and red hooked rug concealed wood floors in need of a new coat of varnish.

The room wasn't as lavish as most of the hotel suites she had occupied, but she finally had a place to call home. She was content with her decision to begin her new life in Oklahoma Territory. She was beginning to feel alive and strong.

As the weeks passed into the heat of summer, Ada continued working hard. She usually spent Sundays with Gwen, Luke, and sometimes Rose. Luke took them to see the different sites around town, but often they shared a lazy day at the boardinghouse.

Luke was always thoughtful and humorous. He was intelligent and kind. Even though he was attentive to her, he was never insolent or presumptuous. She enjoyed his friendship and began to look forward to the times she could be with him.

He surprised her one evening, though, by coming into the shop just before closing time. He entered with hat in hand. He waved at Ada as she looked up from her task.

Mrs. Parkinson peered over her glasses at him. "May I assist you in some way?"

"I was just waitin' for Miss Marsh to leave for the day."

Mrs. Parkinson glanced at the watch pinned to her shirtwaist. "It is closing time, if you would like to go, Miss Marsh."

"Thank you." Ada removed the measuring tape from her shoulders and placed it neatly on the table. She reached underneath for her handbag. She hurried to Luke. He opened the door for her, and they walked out into the warmth of the evening.

"Have you been in town visiting Gwen?"

"No." He smiled as he shook his head. "I was hopin' you would like to have supper with me tonight."

"I'd love to."

"Where would you like to go?"

"I've actually wanted to go to the Norwood restaurant for chicken and dumplings."

"The Norwood it is."

They strolled down Main Street. He was his usual jovial self, but he seemed to have something on his mind.

He slowed his steps. He cleared his throat and

stated, "Ada, I'm sure you realize that I'm more than interested in you."

"Yes." She was wary of the conversation they were about to have.

He took a deep breath, hurrying on. "I'd like to court you."

She paused. She looked up at him and placed a hand on his arm. "Luke, I'm not ready. . . ."

There was eagerness in his expression as he leaned forward. "You're the most amazin' woman I've ever met," he whispered. "I've never felt this way about any other woman. I've fallen hard for you, Ada." His eyes beseeched her. "Give it a chance. Give *me* a chance."

She was stirred by his candor. He'd shared his heart with her in the middle of the sidewalk for all to see. In the past, men had tried to corner her in private until she was compelled to run away. Could she have faith in Luke? Would she dare? Was she destined to live bitterly alone? Or could she finally have the family she had always longed for? The only way to know the answer was to step off what seemed to be a giant precipice. Ultimately, she nodded. "But I'm not promising anything."

"I understand." He moved her hand to the crook of his arm. "I give you my word. I won't coerce you into anything."

"I'll hold you to that, Mr. Logan." The corners of her mouth turned up.

"It's my solemn vow." There was a playful twinkle in his eye as he continued. "But you do realize that you're goin' to marry me someday, Miss Ada, don't you?"

"I wouldn't wait with bated breath," she teased.

He grinned. "I'll wait for an eternity if I have to." He squeezed her hand before they resumed their walk.

She was unsure about accepting his offer of courtship but decided she would take it slowly. She would have plenty of time to weigh the consequences. She knew he would be a gentleman about it if she changed her mind. At least, she hoped he would be.

They arrived at the restaurant minutes later. As they entered, Ada spotted Lilith Carlisle. It was the first time she had encountered the woman since she discovered her with Hugh. She'd known it would be inevitable in a town the size of Shawnee, but she still wasn't quite ready for a meeting.

They had to pass by Lilith and a rather rotund woman. Lilith's companion was graying but lavishly outfitted. Lilith gave them a derisive sniff when they walked by her table.

Anger threatened to bubble over as Ada glared over one shoulder at Lilith's smirking face.

When they were out of earshot, Luke whispered, "If you'd like to go somewhere else . . ."

"I will not," she seethed.

They sat at a table nearby.

"I won't give her the satisfaction of running me off." She stared at the back of Lilith's head. "I can't believe her insolence, her . . . her shamelessness." She leaned forward and said through clenched teeth, "She should be begging my forgiveness. Instead, she sits there like a queen."

Luke reached across the table and ran his thumb across her knuckles. His eyes were full of understanding and compassion. "I know. She's the most immodest woman I've had the misfortune of knowin'. But try not to let her goad you. And don't ever listen to anything she has to say. There's not a truthful bone in her body. It won't do you any good to pay attention to her. I had to learn that the hard way."

She inhaled slowly. He was right. He knew from experience the gall of that girl. She wouldn't let Lilith Carlisle control her emotions.

"I don't know why Mrs. Walker puts up with her." He glanced back at the woman sitting with Lilith.

"Who is she?"

"Her husband is the president of the biggest bank in town. I've heard they're from old money in New

York. She likes to use her influence around town, and the townfolk usually listen."

"Why would she dine with the likes of Lilith Carlisle?"

"Mrs. Walker is the main benefactor of the theater. She wants to nurture the arts in this so-called uncivilized town. Apparently she doesn't much care how or with whom she does it."

Ada gave an unladylike snort. "Well, if she consorts with *that* pretty snake long enough, she's bound to get bitten."

He snickered. "You can bet on that." He picked up the menu. "Now, let's eat. All this grumblin' has made me hungry."

Ada pushed her concerns about Lilith Carlisle aside, but they resurfaced bright and early Monday morning. Mrs. Parkinson was having a sale on all yard goods. The store was bustling with business. There was quite a crowd when Mrs. Walker made a grand entrance.

Ada was closest to the door. She reluctantly went to her and pasted a smile onto her face as she neared. "May I be of assistance?" She pushed a strand of hair out of her eyes.

Mrs. Walker looked down her nose at her. She

raised her weak chin. "Mrs. Parkinson?" she called. Her voice carried over the throng of women.

The shop owner made her way to them. "Yes, Mrs. Walker?" she asked wearily.

"A respectable woman such as yourself surely has not employed a woman with so sullied a reputation." She nodded toward Ada.

Ada gasped. Mrs. Parkinson's face was void of expression.

"This *lady* makes a habit of carrying on with men publicly," Mrs. Walker continued.

All eyes turned to the trio. Loud whispers erupted around them.

Ada's face burned. "I have done no such thing."

"Miss Marsh, would you please assist the lady with the pink ribbons on her hat?" Mrs. Parkinson inclined her head to a young woman at the back of the store. Ada saw that it was Rose. "I will take care of Mrs. Walker."

Ada held her head high as she navigated through the shocked patrons.

"Oh, Ada!" Rose exclaimed. She grasped her hands, pulling her to a quiet corner. "Are you—?"

"I'll be fine." She drew a shaky breath.

"What would possess Mrs. Walker to do such a thing?" Rose looked as if she could cry for Ada.

"I'm sure Lilith Carlisle had something to do with it."

"Oh. I should have known. What are you going to do?"

"I don't know. My future depends upon Mrs. Parkinson."

Rose hugged her. "She'll do the right thing. Now, let's show these hens that you have nothing to be ashamed of. Help me find the perfect material for a new dress. My parents have another gentleman for me to meet. I want to look as lovely as you can make me."

"Oh, Rose." Ada's voice caught in her throat. "I couldn't make you any lovelier than you already are."

The day, even though it was busy, was excruciatingly long. Ada couldn't read Mrs. Parkinson's expression. She realized early on she wouldn't find out her fate until the store closed. She didn't know if that was encouraging or not.

Mrs. Parkinson locked the door, and she turned the OPEN sign around. She faced Ada. She removed her glasses, cleaned them with her blouse, and returned them to her face. "I'm afraid we have some disturbing business to discuss, Miss Marsh." Her eyes bored into her. "As I informed you before you were hired, I expect propriety at all times."

"But I have always behaved with decorum."

"Do you refute the assertion that while you were engaged to one man, you were seen being carried into your hotel room by another man?"

"I. . . ." She gulped. "I had been in an accident. I injured my ankle. Mr. Logan happened to be present. He was concerned for my health, so he did carry me to my room. My former fiancé arrived shortly, as did Dr. Maxwell."

Mrs. Parkinson's lips formed a thin line. "Do you give me your word? You are telling me the truth?"

"Yes." Her heart thudded as she awaited the woman's decision.

"I despise rumors, Miss Marsh. Almost as much as I do the wealthy trying to intimidate me." She gave her a wry smile. "Luckily, my loan is not at Mr. Walker's bank." She patted Ada's shoulder. "It's been a long day, Miss Marsh, and we have another one ahead of us. Let's go home."

Later that evening, when she was in the sanctuary of her room, Ada rummaged through the dresser for her grandmother's Bible. It had been in the bottom of a trunk for years. She knew Gwen had placed it in one of the drawers. It didn't take long to find it. She sat on the floor with it.

She ran her fingertips across the worn black leather. She flipped through the thin pages. Her grandmother had always been fond of the Psalms. She wondered if she would find any solace there. A passage underlined with pencil caught her eye.

She read the words a second time aloud, "Fret not thyself because of evildoers . . . Delight thyself in the Lord; and he shall give thee the desires of thine heart. . . ."

She swallowed hard. Even though she probably hadn't seen the end of Lilith Carlisle's trying to disturb her life, she felt a glimmer of hope. It was some consolation after such a difficult day. She didn't know yet what her heart desired, but she was now more confident that she would get it.

Chapter Twelve

Luke had never been so furious. No one in his whole life had made him as angry as this woman. Lilith. He couldn't believe his ears when Rose stopped him at the mercantile. She informed him about the lies Lilith had told Mrs. Walker, who in turn had spread the gossip as soon as she could at the dress shop. He had dropped his items onto the counter at the store and charged down the street. He'd had enough of Lilith. He would take care of her once and for all. He clenched his fists as he burst through the front door of the theater.

He stalked down the middle aisle. "Lilith! Lilith Carlisle. If you're here, show yourself!" he shouted.

Presently, she sashayed onstage from behind the curtain. "Why, Mr. Logan. What a pleasure," she cooed.

He bounded up the stairs at the left of the stage. "This is no 'pleasure,' believe me," he ground out.

He grabbed her roughly by one arm and pulled her aside, away from any prying ears.

"There's no need to use force with me." She extracted herself from his grip. She eyed him from head to toe. "You're so powerful. It's no wonder you were strong enough to carry that woman all the way to her room."

"Don't play coy with me. You know full well why I was takin' her to her room."

She feigned wide-eyed innocence.

"I've had enough of this. You will leave me and mine alone." He jabbed a forefinger into the air in front of her face.

"She's yours now, is she?" She crossed her arms. "We'll see about that."

He inched closer, so angry that he couldn't speak.

"You lay your hands on me in anger, and I'll have you arrested before you get to the door." She clutched his fingers, drawing them from in front of her face to over her heart. "Unless, of course, you have changed your mind. Then you can manhandle me all you want."

He jerked his hand from her. "I told you in January that I would never—"

"Oh, spare me your self-righteous indignation. No man has ever refused me. Some dirt farmer won't be the first."

"I may be the first, but I'm sure I won't be the last." He turned from her and stomped down the stairs.

"She's old news, Luke." Lilith's voice was icy as it followed him. "Come with me, and hang on to a rising star."

He paused long enough to glower at her. "Never," he sneered. He stood his full height. "Now, leave us alone."

"As you so eloquently put it—never."

He felt as if he was trying to get out of quicksand. He stormed out. It was useless to argue with her, and he couldn't stand to breathe the same air a second longer.

Independence Day promised to be an enjoyable occasion. Mrs. Parkinson closed the shop, so Ada was free to lend a hand at the church bazaar. They were trying to raise more funds to construct the new house of worship.

About midmorning, she rode with Luke and Gwen to the site where the church was to be built. White duck tent tops were pitched in neat rows on the huge lot next to the newly erected two-story rectory. Luke dropped them off, assuring them he would return as soon as the benefit livestock auction at the stockyards to the west was concluded.

Ada and Gwen wandered through the crowd, looking for their stations. They marveled at all the products that had been donated and were now for sale. There were booths of baked goods, furniture, useful articles, and fancywork. There was even a country store selling flour, eggs, and butter. Tables were set up at one end to hawk mouthwatering food. Homemade pretzels, steamed corn on the cob, taffy, cinnamon rolls, and many other tempting items filled the air with their aromas.

Ada dragged Gwen away under protest.

"I'll be back soon," Gwen called out over her shoulder to the women watching the food booths.

"There must be some good cooks represented here." Ada smiled.

"Wonderful," Gwen sighed. "The sausage Mrs. Schiltz makes on bread Mrs. Marak bakes with one of Mrs. Mauldin's dill pickles . . . it's a meal fit for a king."

Ada chuckled. "Find me before you go to this feast. I'll want to join you."

Gwen laughed. "Of course I will." She squinted against the sun. "Look, there's Rose."

They made their way to where Rose was sitting behind a table covered with needlepoint, crocheted doilies, table runners, lace, and other ornamental sewing.

"I'm glad you're here," Rose greeted them. "Mrs. Goodnight just left to go look after the other fancywork booth. I can use the help."

"Mrs. Burke is probably looking for me over at the country store," Gwen said as she stepped away. "I'd better go. I'll see you two later." She saluted them and hurried away.

As she sat down, Ada examined the items on the table, noting there was only one of five fringed shawls she'd made remaining. Business must have been brisk that morning.

"It looks as if sales have been good," Ada commented.

"Yes. But who wouldn't want a shawl stitched by the famous actress Ada Marsh?" Rose asked cheerfully.

"I'm just Ada Marsh now," she tried to protest.

"I wouldn't mind buying the last one myself." Rose fingered the soft pink paisley material.

"There's no need for that. I'll make you one for free."

"It's for a good cause." Rose reached under

the table for her handbag, took out two dollars, and put it into the collection box to make her purchase.

"Oh, Rose, you are a darling." Ada put her arm around her shoulders.

They were interrupted as a shopper approached their booth. A steady stream of customers kept them busy. Before they turned around twice, their shift was over, and their replacements had arrived. Ada and Rose roamed the bazaar in search of Gwen. Instead, they came across Mrs. Dennis.

Rose's mother was a smaller, graying version of her daughter, except that all the years of being an army colonel's wife showed in her countenance. She was friendly enough, although she did tend to be undemonstrative.

Ada knew that Rose respected her parents but wasn't very close to them. It was no wonder she'd made her way through life timidly so far. She didn't have encouraging parents to help her along. It was wonderful that she was beginning to blossom by using her musical gifts.

"I'm glad I found you, dear," Mrs. Dennis said. "Your father isn't feeling well. We should take him home, out of this heat."

"Of course, Mother."

"I hate to ask, Miss Marsh, but I was watching the lemonade table. Could you relieve me?"

"I'd be glad to."

"Thank you." She nodded her appreciation, then hurried away with Rose on her heels.

Ada found the lady in charge and told her she was there to take Mrs. Dennis' place. She had been there a good hour when Luke arrived.

His hair was damp around the edges, and his collar was soggy.

"Been working hard, have you?" she asked playfully.

He handed her a coin and accepted the glass she gave him. He took a long swig before answering. "Well, Miss Ada, it's like this. A couple of fellas and I didn't want to offend our lady friends, so we cleaned up at the pump over yonder." He tugged at his wet collar. "I just wish I'd had the brains to change my shirt *after* I washed up."

She laughed as she shook her head.

He leaned over the table. "So, how long do you have to stay here?"

"I might be persuaded to leave. I think reinforcements have arrived."

"Good." He drained his glass, and he set it to one side. "Let's go."

He extended his arm. She took it with pleasure.

She noted the looks of longing from other girls as they passed. Apparently, they thought Luke was quite a catch. She had to admit, she agreed with them. He was rather handsome.

They meandered through the displays. They ended up at an impromptu stage with a crowd gathering around. Reverend Schneider was standing at the edge of the platform with a boy who was holding a large jar filled with tickets. Various items were exhibited behind them.

The clergyman held his hands up to silence the group. "We're ready to have the raffle. I'd ask that you wait to claim your prize until the end. And, to insure that no one thinks I've tampered with the results, young Timothy here is going to draw the names."

Everyone chuckled. Someone playfully heckled the young minister.

"Now, John, I'll expect to see you in the first row on Sunday."

Laughter sprinkled the crowd. Everyone quieted down when Reverend Schneider told Timothy to draw the first name. He read names until the toilet set, chiffonier, photograph album, and Angora goat were raffled off.

"Now, the last item is an engraved silver bracelet donated by Mr. Carroll's mercantile, and the winner is . . . Luke Logan."

There were several whistles as Luke raised his hand. He made his way to the stage with the other winners. He tucked the bracelet into his pants pocket with a sheepish grin.

He returned to Ada. "I sure am disappointed," he commented, wagging his head.

"You are?"

His face broke out into a smile. "Yeah. I was really wantin' that goat."

Chapter Thirteen

As dusk neared, Luke drove Ada down Kick-apoo to the fairgrounds, where fireworks were go-ing to be on display. Gwen volunteered to help close the fund-raiser and assured them she could find some generous soul to take her home. Luke had to admit he was mighty tickled to have some time alone with Ada.

He pulled up with the other wagons and buggies at the edge of the fairgrounds. Ada removed her straw hat. She put the menacing pin back through the crown, placed it on the seat between them, and fluffed her upswept hair. Even after a long, swelter-ing day, she appeared cool and unruffled. She was wearing his favorite dress. He hadn't seen her in the gauzy white gown since the day she found Hugh Wellington with Lilith.

"You look lovely in that dress," he complimented her.

He must have caught her by surprise, because she seemed flustered as she brushed at the skirt. "The hem is dingy, and I'm all wrinkled."

"You look as fresh as a newly opened rose." He reached out and ran the back of one forefinger along her cheek.

He could see her struggling to decide whether to accept his familiar behavior or not. He dropped his hand and dug into his pocket. He held out the silver bracelet. "I'd like for you to have this."

"Oh, Luke, you shouldn't—"

"When I bought my chances, I hoped I could win it for you." He held her eyes with his.

She consented. She showed her pleasure as he slipped the bracelet over her delicate hand. "It's fine workmanship." She admired it and returned his gaze. "Thank you."

"It's my pleasure." He squeezed her hand, and he turned his attention to their surroundings. "I think we'll have a better view from over there." He nodded toward a stand of trees, away from the majority of people.

"That's fine with me."

He helped her down and placed her hand in the crook of his arm. They strolled over to the spot and found several other couples whispering to each other. Cicadas serenaded them. Fireflies flickered around them.

"The sounds of summer," he mused aloud.

"I barely remember my parents or the farm in Missouri that I was born on, but I'll never forget the summers. I would run barefoot through the fields, braids flying, trying to catch fireflies. I used to think that if I caught one, I could tie its legs together and have a sparkling ring."

He chuckled. "Did you ever catch any?"

"No." She sighed. "But I'm sure it was for the betterment of the species."

"Maybe you'll get that sparkling ring someday."

"Perhaps," she commented. "Oh, look at that." She pointed to the first fireworks exploding in the darkened sky.

She had effectively changed the course of their conversation. He couldn't tell if that was purposeful or not. He'd promised not to press her, though, so he would have to try to follow her lead. It wasn't going to be easy.

He stood behind her as they watched the dazzling explosions. They were both in awe of the brilliance and variety of designs. At one particularly showy flash, he placed his hands on her shoulders. He bent to her ear. "Did you like that one?"

"It was amazing," she whispered.

She inclined her head to his. He couldn't stop himself from trailing one thumb along her soft neck. She shivered.

"Are you cold?"

"No," she said softly. She took his hands and wrapped his arms around her. She leaned into him.

He drew in the soft scent of her. "I'm glad you're in my life, Ada."

"So am I, Luke," she murmured as she rested her head on his chest. "So am I."

Ada knew she was in trouble. Serious trouble. Her so-called resolve had fled as soon as the first handsome man came calling. All her intentions had toppled like a house of cards at Luke's slightest touch that evening. She knew she was falling for him.

When he brought her home, she jumped out of his buggy and ran up the stairs like a child before he had time to blink. She could see the confusion on his face as she waved to him and let herself into the house. She walked quietly up the stairs and into the darkness of her room. She turned on the electric light. She plopped onto the bed, which protested with a loud squeak.

How could she have those spine-tingling feelings for both Luke and Hugh? How could one be right and the other wrong? She was too confused. She didn't trust herself.

She had made one heartbreaking mistake, and she didn't want to do it again. She knew that Luke was different from Hugh. He was kind. He was amusing and full of brawn and vigor. They weren't made of the same cloth, but she still felt uneasy.

She was curious if Gwen would have any advice about her situation. Gwen was engaged, after all.

She had seen a light shining out from under her door when she came up, so Gwen was awake. She might as well go talk to her. She got up and went next door. She rapped lightly.

"Come in," Gwen invited.

Ada entered and found her scribbling away at her small desk.

"I'm sorry. If you're working, I can come another time."

"Oh, no." Gwen pushed the paper aside and put the lid on the ink bottle. "I finished my article about the church bazaar. I was just writing to Mother to tell her I'll be coming home for a visit next month."

"When are you leaving?" Ada sat in a rocking chair nearby.

"I'll wait until after Luke's birthday on August nineteenth."

Ada made a mental note of that information before she asked, "How long are you going to be gone?"

"Several weeks. My mother and Walter have been insisting for quite a while."

"Your fiancé . . . what is he like?"

"Walter?" She grinned. "I've been told by more than one disappointed maiden that he's quite a catch." She stroked her chin with ink-stained fingers. "He's a big strapping fellow with blond hair and gray eyes. He has the physique of a blacksmith, like his father, but he worked his way through law school. He's been an attorney in Guthrie for a few years."

"How did you meet him?"

"A couple of years ago, my mother decided I should meet this fine gentleman. She invited him to tea." She smiled. "He's been by my side ever since."

"When are you going to marry?"

"I'm not sure. Walter wants to right away. I was lucky that he agreed to let me come to Shawnee for a year. He thought the change would prepare me for settling down." She grimaced. "My year will be up soon. I don't know if I'm ready yet or not."

"What are you going to do?"

"I'm not sure. That's why I'm returning for a while." She leaned forward. "I love writing. I'm excited about my job, but I have ideas for a novel. I'd like to try to write it. I'm hoping Walter will let me stay another year so I can. He's been more than patient, though. I don't know if he will want to wait any longer." She sighed.

"Sounds as if you have a dilemma on your hands also." She had to ask her. It was now or never. "Gwen, how did you know that Walter was the one? The one you trusted enough to spend the rest of your life with?"

Gwen shrugged. "I'm not sure how to explain it. I guess I just love him." Her eyes sparkled. "Why do you ask? Are you and Luke—"

"Don't get too excited." She gave her a wry smile. "I really enjoy Luke. I have a great . . . attraction to him."

"Then why do you look so disturbed?"

"It scares me. I'm not sure I trust—"

"You don't trust him?" Gwen's eyebrows shot up.

"No . . . I don't trust myself. My judgment of men hasn't been good."

Gwen looked perplexed.

"There are these . . . feelings that arise when you're close to a man," she tried to explain.

"Oh. Oh, sure." Gwen nodded.

"I had this attraction to Hugh, and he was a fraud. How can I know that those kinds of emotions for Luke are right?"

Gwen cleared her throat and gazed at her reflection in the dark window. "I don't know. I . . . couldn't say I have that kind of ardor for Walter. I just assumed that would come after marriage." She turned back to Ada. "But what I do know is that you can trust Luke. I don't think he's ever been so smitten with any other woman. I can see it plain as day. He loves you, Ada."

Ada nodded while she reflected on Gwen's observations. "I want to believe what he's telling me. He says I'm the first to affect him this way. It's difficult to imagine, though, that a man as handsome as Luke hasn't been involved with anyone before."

"Believe me, I would know. He couldn't keep a secret like that from me." Gwen grinned.

Ada took a deep breath. "I'll take your word, but I may need encouragement from time to time. It's not going to be easy for me to give my heart away again . . . even to him."

Gwen hugged her. "I'll be here for you anytime."

Chapter Fourteen

July was scorching. Business was slow in town. Rose and her parents escaped to the Colorado Rockies to stay with some relatives. They hoped the cooler air would rejuvenate the colonel's health.

Even though the weather was almost unbearable, Ada enjoyed her walks to and from work. The stroll was comfortable in the mornings. The milk deliveryman drove past her at the same spot every day and doffed his hat to her. A tidy neighbor lady who shook out a colorfully braided rug at the same time always waved to her. The shop owners along Bell Street acknowledged her as they prepared for their workdays.

Her new routine was a balm to her soul. She was

beginning to feel like a part of the community. She had never felt so alive or so robust in constitution.

A reprieve from the heat came at the beginning of August with a thunderstorm. It brought a little moisture to the thirsty soil and temperatures down to tolerable low nineties.

Ada spent her evenings sewing curtains for Luke for his birthday. She found the perfect green brocade to complement the sofa in his parlor. For the bedrooms she chose filmy muslin with blue stripes, and for the kitchen she bought red gingham.

Making items for his home felt like an intimate gesture. It was a step she thought she was finally prepared to take. Silent prayers of anticipation went into every stitch.

On the morning of Luke's birthday, Ada heard loud voices in the hall outside her room. There was a knock on Gwen's door, and Gwen squealed. Ada fastened the last button on her green skirt and cracked her door open. She saw men, women, and children crowded in the corridor.

"What are you all doing here?" Gwen asked with glee.

"We're here to take you to Luke's for his birthday," an older gentleman responded.

"Came in on the train from Guthrie this morning," a younger man announced.

"Rented some surreys from the livery," another commented.

"Are you going to let us in, dear heart, or do we languish out here until you're ready?" A rather large, well-dressed, blond man spoke up.

"Walter! I didn't notice you and Mother back there." She took in the sight of one and all, then spotted Ada. "Ada, come here and meet the family."

Ada widened the door with aplomb, trying to ignore the fact that she had been spying on them. She smiled and stepped forward.

"Everyone, this is Ada Marsh. She's a dear friend of mine"—there was a twinkle in her eye as she continued—"and Luke's."

"*The* Ada Marsh?" a boy of about ten asked, his eyes as wide as saucers.

"Yes, Oliver," Gwen informed him with a grin. She waved to the three fine-looking men who resembled Luke. "These are Luke's older brothers— Mark, John, and Peter—and Peter's wife, Enid, and their children."

Hands were shaken and pleasantries exchanged.

"And Luke's parents."

The dignified couple moved forward. She could see a spark of Luke's playfulness in Mr. Logan's countenance as he greeted her. Mrs. Logan was a petite woman with an inviting face.

She held her hands out to Ada. "Luke's written so much about you. I feel I know you, dear." She squeezed Ada's hands. "He was right. He could never describe your beauty in a letter."

"Thank you, Mrs. Logan." Ada felt her color rise. She'd blushed more this year than she had in her entire life.

"This is my mother and my Walter," Gwen said with her fingers resting on his arm.

"It's nice to meet you both," Ada said.

"Of course, the pleasure is ours, Miss Marsh." Walter gave her a practiced smile and turned to Gwen. "Are you ready, Gwendolyn? We haven't all day. We are returning on the train this evening."

"I just need to put on my hat. Come in. It'll only take a minute."

While everyone filed into Gwen's room, Ada returned to her own. She checked to see if her hair was pinned securely. She placed a straw hat with a green silk band atop her head and put the hat pin through. She grabbed Luke's large present, wishing that it wasn't so conspicuous. She hadn't realized she would be traveling to his place among strangers.

She joined the others. The entire group piled into the surreys, and they were on their way. Ada settled between Enid and Mrs. Logan. Enid held the youngest of her five children in her lap. Ada thought the girl was about four, and her name was Mercy. Luke's brothers sat in the front, joking and carrying on the entire time. The ride passed quickly with them on-board.

"Don't let these brutes scare you off, Miss Marsh," Enid confided as the buggy rolled to a stop at Luke's back door. "They can be civilized when need be." She raised her voice for her husband to hear. "And I do believe Luke is the most gallant of them all."

"I heard that, woman." Peter reached for Mercy and put her down. He lifted Enid out and twirled her around.

She shrieked and then whispered into his ear before he let her feet touch solid ground. He kissed her cheek before releasing her.

Ada was warmed as she watched their display of affection. After many years of marriage and several children, they were still obviously in love. She wondered if she could have that someday. Was Luke the one to share it with?

John took her package, and Mark helped her down.

The screen door opened, and Luke stepped out. A broad grin lit up his bronzed face. His damp hair was combed into place.

"What's all this excitement?" he asked as he buttoned a cuff.

Little Mercy ran to him, skirts flying, and jumped into his arms. "It's your birfday, Uncle Luke."

He squeezed her and kissed the top of her brown, curly hair. His eyes scanned his family until they rested on Ada. His smile changed for her. Her heart fluttered at his acknowledgment. Perhaps Luke *was* the one her soul longed for.

He broke their gaze and offered, "Well, come on in, everyone. I'm glad you're all here."

The day was a treat for Ada. The casual, jolly spirit of Luke's big family was alluring. They enveloped her into their midst and treated her as one of their own. Their kindness made her mourn the loss of her parents, but it also made her long for a family of her own.

She watched Luke have serious conversations with his nieces and nephews. He was patient and listened to every word they had to say. He would be a wonderful father.

Mrs. Logan, Mrs. Sanders, and Enid came well prepared for a party. They had stopped at the mercantile that morning and purchased enough food for an army. Ada had to pry her attention from Luke to help them get lunch on.

After everyone ate, Mrs. Logan brought out a box that she had carried on the train. It contained Luke's favorite chocolate cake. Pieces were cut and passed around while his nieces gave him his presents.

They helped him open them and gave the appropriate amounts of praise as each one was admired and laid aside. He received handkerchiefs with his initials embroidered in the corner, a new pocketknife, red suspenders, and a book of poetry. He opened Ada's gift last, the children exclaiming over the size of it. All the hours of hard work were worth it when he locked eyes with Ada and mouthed his thanks.

The Logan clan decided to leave early in the afternoon to ensure they would catch their train. Luke invited Ada to stay behind and offered to take her home later. She accepted without a second thought. She was surprised, though, when Gwen informed her she would be leaving, also.

"I just assumed you would stay too," Ada whispered to her. They held back on the porch while the rest were preparing to depart.

"I decided to go back to Guthrie with them."

"I thought you were leaving next week."

"I was, but Walter bought me a ticket for tonight." She seemed pleased as she glanced at him.

"What about the newspaper?"

"Apparently, Walter telephoned Mr. Jennings yesterday. He agreed to let me go a week early." There was a hint of irritation in her eyes, but she continued to smile.

"Well, I guess there's nothing else to say except to wish you a wonderful time."

"It will be." She embraced her quickly. "I have to go home and throw some things into a trunk. I'll be back in a few weeks." She rushed down the steps and climbed into the buggy. Everyone waved as they pulled away.

For a split second, Ada wanted to flee with them. She knew it was cowardice on her part. She braced herself and turned to face her imagined foe.

Luke was standing at the bottom of the steps. His arms were crossed over his chest. He gave her a lopsided grin. "I'm not that scary, am I?"

The corners of her mouth turned up, and she said wryly, "You have no idea."

He chuckled and held a hand out to her. "How about we go for a walk?"

"I'd love to."

She took his arm. They strolled down a trail worn through the woods. The shade helped to stave off some of the heat of the day. They paused when they came to a deep ravine cut into red clay. Rust-colored water trickled over the rocky creek bed. They stood under an old pecan tree, watching and listening to the moving water.

"So, what do you think of my family?"

"I enjoyed them. And I can see why you were enchanted with Enid," she teased.

He waved a hand. "That was a long time ago." He positioned himself in front of her. "I never thought she was as lovely as you."

She couldn't meet his gaze. Negative thoughts filtered back into her head. She wanted to dismiss them, but she could not stop herself. "Is that all I am to you? A pretty actress to have on your arm?" she asked quietly.

"Of course not." He took her by the shoulders, forcing her to look into his wounded eyes. "I think you're kind, spunky, and talented. You're an appealin' woman. Inside and out."

She accepted his sincerity. She placed a hand on his hard chest. He was unflinching and solid. Her breath quickened along with his. She could feel his heart thudding beneath his shirt. His cleanly shaved jaw clenched. His chiseled lips seemed poised to speak. His eyes pierced all the way through her.

"You have my heart in your hand, Ada," he murmured. "You've had it for a long time."

She couldn't utter a word.

"Do I have some comer of yours?"

"Yes," she breathed.

He bent forward. His lips found hers. His kiss was

tentative and soft. She leaned toward him. He wrapped her into his arms, his mouth lingering on hers.

He moaned and pulled away. "I'd better take you home."

Words were hopeless. She only nodded. Her fate was locked, and Luke held the key.

Chapter Fifteen

Ada was happy. She was afraid to admit it to herself, but she was. Her high spirits had everything to do with Luke Logan. He was an exquisite curiosity. He was a maverick in contrast to every other man she had known. All of that made him extremely enticing. She looked forward to learning more about him and what made him the man he was. At last, she was ready to enjoy him.

At the end of August, Luke invited her to a concert at the opera house. She was excited to have an elegant evening out. It called for a new gown. She knew right away that she wanted the dark burgundy taffeta silk she had been eyeing at Mrs. Parkinson's.

She spent a pretty penny but knew the results would be worth it.

She stitched well into the night for several days. The lack of sleep and her sore fingers didn't deter her enthusiasm as she admired her handiwork. The off-the-shoulder neckline was outlined by tiny jet beads. The loose-fitting bodice was topped with tight half-sleeves with more jet sewn on. The long skirt flared gracefully at the floor.

She was delighted by her efforts. She couldn't wait to see Luke's face when she wore it. She knew she wouldn't be disappointed by his reaction.

With a recently purchased derby hat in hand, Luke knocked on the front door of the boarding-house. Mrs. Brown let him in.

"Why, Mr. Logan, don't you look jest fine and dandy?" She chuckled.

"Thank you, Mrs. Brown." He inserted a finger in his new collar, hoping he wouldn't choke to death before the night was over. He straightened his white bow tie.

"I'll go on up and see if Miss Marsh is ready. You can go on into the parlor and sit a spell."

He nodded. He watched her trudge up the stairs, apparently in no hurry at all. He went into the room at the right of the entryway. It was blessedly empty. He was too tense to sit. He paced the length of the worn Oriental carpet.

He hoped he looked presentable enough. He had dug through his closet and found a black cutaway frock coat that he hadn't worn since Peter's wedding. He'd dusted off his black leather oxfords and starched his good white shirt. It was too late now to wish he'd bought a new suit.

He heard Mrs. Brown chattering. He stepped out of the parlor. Mrs. Brown stood aside to let Ada descend.

He was totally and utterly speechless. A black comb nestled in her upswept hair. A silver filigree choker with dangling garnets encircled the graceful curves of her neck. The exquisite gown set off her alabaster complexion. Over long black silk gloves, she wore the bracelet he had given her. A black lace fan hung from her other wrist.

He knew his eyeballs must have been popping out of his head as she rustled toward him. He felt like a schoolboy, all jittery inside.

"Good evening, Luke," Ada greeted him. Her voice sounded softer and lower than usual.

He had to clear his throat twice before words would come. "Ada . . ." he murmured. "You are simply amazing."

Sandra Wilkins

She smiled her pleasure. She appraised him with appreciation. "So are you, Mr. Logan."

Ada was on his arm as they entered the opera house. Some people stared and whispered among themselves, while others greeted them warmly. They made their way through the lobby and down the aisle to their seats in the second row.

It wasn't long before the lights dimmed. The orchestra from Oklahoma City began the first strains of Schubert's Symphony no. 5.

"I love this composition," she whispered.

He inclined his head toward her. His shoulder brushed hers. Even in the low light, he could see tiny goose bumps rise on her flesh. The faint scent of her perfume mingled with the elaborate music. He closed his eyes to absorb it all. His heart swelled with the ascent of the flutes and violins. He would never forget how this felt, this being in love.

At intermission, they followed the crowd to the lobby. He steered her to a quiet corner while he went for refreshments.

He was returning to her, when Lilith cut him off. He almost spilled the punch because of her abruptness. He eyed her suspiciously.

"I see you and that dressed-up trollop are having a romantic evening." Her speech was slurred.

The alcohol on her breath almost knocked him over. "You've been at it a while." He motioned to the drinks in his hands. "You'd better try somethin' a little less potent."

"I'm not drunk," she hissed.

"You are, and I'm not goin' to stand here and listen to your insults." He tried to pass by.

"Run on back to her." She swayed but stayed upright. "She'll get tired of you soon enough. You just wait and see."

He snorted at her words. He walked away, shaking his head to rid his mind of her. He rounded the corner. Men and women mingled around Ada. A few were trying to make polite conversation with her. She seemed distracted, though. When he neared, she turned to him and beamed. It took his breath away.

"I had a wonderful evening, Luke," Ada told him as he walked her to Mrs. Brown's porch.

She could see him well in the light of the full moon. She had never laid eyes on a more handsome man. She had been hard pressed all night to keep from gawking at him.

"I'll always remember it." He backed against a porch post, jamming his hands into his pockets. There was yearning in the dark pools of his eyes.

"I'll never forget the way you looked tonight . . . or how I feel about you."

"And how is that?" She couldn't resist the question.

"You know full well." He smirked. "I'm not sure you're ready to hear it yet. I think I'll just keep it to myself for now."

"If you must." She raised an eyebrow.

"Be warned, though, I'll be more charmin' than ever," he teased. "You won't stand a chance."

She smiled. "Then don't be alarmed when I fall head over heels. It will be entirely your fault."

"I'll readily take the blame." He held his arms out to her.

She stepped into the security of him. She rested her cheek on his rough lapel, inhaling the combination of shaving soap and wool. She sighed.

"What's on your mind?" he asked quietly.

"I feel . . . safe . . . for the first time in my life." She pulled back to search his face, but not so far that she was out of his grasp. "In the back of my mind, I always longed for a home and a family of my own. But the profession I was in made me think it was impossible. It's difficult to believe this could be a reality for me. . . . Do you understand what I'm trying to say?"

He nodded. "I was one who always liked to be on my own. I liked some excitement. I moved from one job to the next. But I was ready to settle down when I homesteaded here. I thought I had it all—until I met you. I realized how empty life is without someone to share it with."

"Doesn't this seem too good to be true?"

"I know this may be hard for you, Ada, but don't get scared and run away. I don't think I could handle that." His voice cracked with emotion.

"It's not easy for me," she admitted.

He moved his hands to her shoulders and held her firmly. "It's just you, me, and the truth out here on this porch. You can trust me. If you'll only believe, your broken heart can be whole again."

His openness did begin to mend her heart, stitch by stitch. She stretched up, touched his jaw, and kissed him. He responded eagerly, sincerely.

She slowly moved from his embrace. "I believe," she whispered.

Chapter Sixteen

On the spur of the moment, Luke saddled Daisy. He had made plans to see Ada the following evening, but he didn't want to wait that long.

Ada sure did entrance him. He felt wobbly, weak, and strong all at the same time when he was with her. He hoped it wouldn't be long before he could ask her to marry him. She was beginning to reach out to him, but she was still as skittish as a green horse. He didn't want to frighten her away. He knew he would have to wait a little while longer. In the meantime, he had to see her as often as he could.

He put a boot into the stirrup and swung his other leg over. He took his seat and patted the mare's neck. "Let's go, girl. Let's see how you do in town today." She pranced in place, straining on the bit. "I hope you're ready for this."

He clucked his tongue. The horse shot forward, and they set off in a questionable trot.

Mrs. Parkinson left early in the day with a headache. Ada was alone when she closed the shop. She had tidied up the last table when she heard a rap on the door.

She saw Lilith Carlisle standing there. Lilith beckoned, and Ada reluctantly walked to the door.

"Let me in, Ada Marsh," she beseeched through the glass. "I need to talk to you." She looked over her shoulder as if she was afraid someone would see her. Her hair was disheveled, and the collar of her white shirtwaist was torn.

Ada was tempted to turn on her heel and ignore her. Curiosity won out, though. She unlocked the door and let her in.

"What do you want, Lilith?" She crossed her arms.

"I came to warn you about Luke, as one thespian to another," she said, trying to catch her breath.

"After the warm reception you gave me, I'm sure I'll accept every word." The sarcasm in her voice was sharp even to her own ears.

There was a flash of emotion in Lilith's eyes before

she continued. "I just wanted to tell you to stay away from him."

"I'm not going to stand here and listen to some jealous tirade." She stared at her evenly. "I'm not some delicate flower you can trample on."

"I didn't come here out of spite. I just wanted to save you from my fate." Lilith placed a shaky hand on her neck. "I was just coming out of the Norwood when Luke accosted me. He pulled me into the alley and told me my little flirtation with Hugh Wellington had been eating away at him. He said he couldn't stand the thought of me with anyone but him." She rubbed her upper arms and flinched from the pain.

Ada's heart was beginning to drop.

"He was getting rough. I told him to stop. . . . He said he knew that actresses were used to being treated worse than that." Tears formed in her eyes. "He said he was tired of your being all high-and-mighty. He didn't want to wait for you anymore. He told me he'd always wanted me, anyway." She shuddered. "I don't know what would have happened if I hadn't gotten away."

There was a roar in Ada's ears. She was afraid she was going to be sick.

"He threatened me before I ran off. He told me if I ever told anyone about this, he would say I was lying.

And he would ruin my career in the process. After all, he's a respected farmer, and I'm just an actress. Who would believe me? If you asked him now, I'm sure he'd deny everything."

Ada tried to inhale much-needed air.

"I was on my way to the police station when I saw you still here. I just had to tell you. I've seen how much time you're spending together. He seems so sincere, but he puts on a better show than P.T. Barnum ever has. I had to let you know what kind of man he really is."

All Ada could do was point to the door. Lilith gave her a sympathetic look and left as abruptly as she had come.

Ada felt as if she had been punched in the stomach. She sank to the floor. She didn't want to believe the woman, but Lilith was actually going to the police. Luke had lied to her. He had lied about everything.

Luke rode Daisy around the corner to the dress shop just in time to see Lilith rush out. He wondered what kind of business she could have had there.

He pulled up, climbed down, and looped the reins around a hitching post. He sauntered to the door, pushed it, and it opened.

He stuck his head in but didn't see anyone. "Ada?"

He heard an odd, strangled sound. He peered around one of the tables. Ada was sitting on the floor with her head in her hands.

"Ada, darlin'. What's wrong?"

She started at his words as if she had been struck. She scooted back as he neared.

"Ada. Has someone hurt you?"

She looked wretched. He reached for her. She scrambled away on her hands and knees. He grabbed after her, and she kicked him in the shin. The surprise of it made him topple onto her. She squirmed furiously as he attempted to subdue her.

"It's me. Everything will be fine now." He tried to soothe her.

"Let go of me," she ground out through clenched teeth.

He reluctantly released her. He helped her to rise, but she quickly shook his hands from her.

She put a trembling hand to strands of her hair that had escaped their pins. Her back was as straight as a rod. She seemed to be studying something on the wall behind him.

"What is wrong?" He was more than confused by her behavior. He wanted to help her, if only she would let him.

"I'm calling your bluff."

"What is that supposed to mean?" He didn't know where this was going, but he had a sinking feeling he wasn't going to like it.

"If you care for me"—she gulped—"as you say you do, you will leave me alone."

"Well, if you're havin' a bad day, all you had to do was ask me to leave." He leaned down to kiss her cheek, but she turned her head. He cleared his throat. "Well . . . I'll see you tomorrow."

"No." Her lips were pressed so hard together, they were white.

"Sunday, then."

"No." She still wouldn't look at him. "Never again."

He couldn't believe his ears. He felt as if she had ripped his heart out of his chest. There was an ache where it once had been. He found his voice somehow. "What are you saying?"

"You told me once that you wouldn't push me. I'm telling you now that I have changed my mind. I'm not interested in you after all. You were an amusing dalliance. I apologize if you are overly fond of me. As I said, if you care for me at all, you will behave as a gentleman and leave me alone."

It was an impressive speech. She almost convinced him, but something wasn't quite right. Her eyes. She hadn't ever looked at him.

He placed his hands on her shoulders. She cringed. "Look me in the eye and tell me that."

Apparently with much effort, she brought pained emerald eyes to his. "Just leave . . . leave and go after Lilith. . . . If you apologize, maybe she won't have you arrested."

"What does Lilith have to do with this?"

She shrugged away from his touch. "I'm sure you know."

"How could I? It's as if I walked in on the third act of a play, and no one wants to tell me what's happened so far." He held his open hands in front of her, closed them, and then dropped his arms.

"Go." She seemed drained.

"Fine." She'd finally gotten his dander up. "But you're not goin' to quit me so easily." He stormed to the door. "This isn't over."

Ada wasn't sure her watery legs could carry her home. She thought about riding the trolley, but she couldn't face the curious glances from the other passengers. She would just have to make her way under her own power.

She waited until Luke had been gone quite a while before she locked the door behind her and set out for home. She went to Main Street the long way, so she might avoid meeting him. She didn't want another confrontation with him.

She felt betrayed and beaten. She had only been kidding herself that Luke was different. She'd only known him a few months. How could she expect any other outcome?

Chapter Seventeen

Luke reined his horse up in front of the Norwood. The animal skidded to a stop and stepped sideways as he jumped down. He threw the reins over the post. He charged into the hotel. Patrons gave him odd looks as his boot heels thundered across the floor.

He spotted Lilith hurrying across the lobby. He caught her before she could get onto the elevator.

"Come here." He grabbed her arm and pulled her to a quiet corner by the stairway.

"Why, Luke, what a surprise." She gave him a saucy smile.

He released his hold and stood looming over her.

"What can I do for you this fine day?" she asked flirtatiously. She ignored his all too obvious rage.

146

"What have you been up to?" he asked angrily.

"Me?" she asked innocently.

"Why were you at the dress shop?"

"You seem miffed, Luke. Been visiting your ladylove? She has you all in a dither." She tilted her head and raised her eyebrows.

He wasn't going to tolerate her attempt to avoid the reason for his visit. "Why were you there? What did you say to her?"

"So many questions. Come on up to my room, and maybe I'll answer a few." She twirled toward the stairwell.

"If you take one step up those stairs, I'll make sure you never work in this town again," he warned.

Apparently, that threat did the trick. She tossed her mane of hair, threw her shoulders back, and slowly turned around. A look of contempt crossed her features.

"You should have seen the look on her face," she said, as cold as ice. "I deserve a standing ovation for that performance."

"What did you do?" He was losing any drop of patience he had left.

With an arrogant lift to her chin, she asked, "She didn't tell you? She's more of a fool than I thought. But, as I said, I was brilliant as the frightened victim of your shameful advances."

He suddenly noticed her ripped blouse and tousled hair. There was no telling what terrible things she had said about him. She sickened him.

"You lying—"

"I don't know why you're angry at me. You should thank me for testing her loyalty. She obviously had none."

He had had enough. He couldn't be near her another second. "You'd better hope you don't meet your Maker anytime soon, or you'll be burnin' in hell."

"Is that a threat?" She bristled.

"Just the truth."

He pivoted from her vileness and sped away to search for Ada.

She knew he was there, even before he spoke her name. Her leaden feet wouldn't take her any farther. Luke's steps pounded the earth toward her. He took her aside to the shade of a cottonwood tree just off Main Street.

He looked haggard and disheveled. She had never seen such confusion or grief in a man. If only it was real.

"I need to talk with you." His voice was shaky. "Lilith boasted about what she'd done. She was under the impression you believed her."

She watched him in silence.

"Don't you know me by now? Have I ever been anything but honorable?"

She struggled to process what he was saying.

"Why would I want someone like her? She is despicable . . . she's manipulative . . ." he sputtered.

Surely she hadn't been duped, had she?

"I would never lay my hands on her that way. You believe that, don't you?" His eyes burned into her.

He seemed so genuine. A wave of mortification and fear washed over her. What had she done?

"I guess she's a better actress than I gave her credit for." He was stiff in demeanor.

"I. . . ." She didn't know what to say. How could she even begin to apologize?

"Even so. . . ." His voice cracked. "Even so, how could you imagine that of me?" His long fingers splayed across his chest.

She wanted to fall at his feet and beg his forgiveness. The betrayal and pain in his eyes seared her. She was unworthy to look at him. She dropped her eyes.

"Fine. If you still feel that way, I'll leave." He took a step away.

"Luke, wait." She panicked. She couldn't let him leave without giving him an explanation. She touched his arm. "I'm so horribly ashamed." Tears threatened to fall. "I . . . I don't know what came over me. She fed my insecurities. . . . I was so wrong. Please . . . can you forgive me?"

He wagged his head. "I don't know, Ada. This is big. I don't know if I can get past it or not."

She didn't know any other way to express her sorrow. She waited awkwardly.

He sighed. He looked so tired. "I'll talk to you later. I can't now."

He trudged across the street to his horse. He swung into the saddle. He gave her one last glance before he urged his horse ahead.

She didn't think anything about the trolley groaning and rattling up Main Street until his horse whinnied. Luke struggled to keep it under control. It shot forward. He grabbed for the pommel, but his grip slid as the horse bucked. He crashed to the ground. He raised his right arm in defense as the horse's hooves struck his midriff. He rolled away and curled into a ball.

Ada wasn't sure if the screams that pierced her ears were from herself or the horse as it scrambled away from Luke and into the path of the trolley. The horse tripped on the track, floundered, and went down as the trolley screeched to a halt. It got to its feet and limped away, head low. A passerby took the reins and stroked its lathered shoulder.

Ada scurried to Luke. She stumbled as she came to him and fell onto her knees next to him. Her muddled, slow-moving mind gave way to vivid reality. His face was too pale. The blood that trickled from the gash on his forehead and oozed from his arm was too red. The perfect imprint of a horseshoe marred his sky blue shirt.

Several men rushed to her aid.

"Let's take him to Mrs. Brown's." She stood. "And . . . please, someone go for Dr. Maxwell."

The strangers hoisted him up and carried him with watchful steps. His limp arms dangled.

She couldn't watch his lifeless body, so she ran ahead. She shouted for Mrs. Brown as she burst through the door. The landlady appeared from the dining room. Ada explained what had happened. They quickly made a pallet of quilts on the floor in the parlor in front of the empty fireplace just as the men brought Luke in. They carefully placed him on the blankets. They stood around in silence as Ada knelt beside him.

"Luke." She bent to his ear. With shaky fingers, she gingerly touched his cheek. "Luke. Speak to me. Wake up. I can't lose you. Please. . . ." The words strangled in her throat. Tears dropped from her face to his.

The mantel clock ticked away the minutes. Dr. Maxwell finally arrived. He was huffing and wiping his brow with a large pristine handkerchief as he entered. The small crowd parted to let him through.

He eased down beside Luke. He opened Luke's eyelids and peered at him through his spectacles. He felt for a pulse. He listened to his chest with a stethoscope. He unbuttoned Luke's shirt and systematically pressed on his flesh.

Luke groaned and flinched when the doctor came to his right side. Dr. Maxwell continued his examination until he was satisfied. He pulled a small bottle of smelling salts out of his black bag. He waved it under Luke's nostrils.

Luke's eyelids fluttered. His eyes barely opened.

"Can you tell me your name?" the doctor asked.

"Luke," he whispered.

"What month is it?"

"August."

"Where do you live?"

"Near Shawnee. . . ." His eyelids closed.

Dr. Maxwell nodded thoughtfully. He faced Ada. "Miss Marsh, he has a concussion and at least two fractured ribs. He could be unconscious for a day or two. You'll need to watch him closely. Elevate his head with a few pillows, and wake him every hour. See if he can answer a few questions."

She nodded.

"I'll strap his ribs with bandages. It doesn't appear that his broken ribs punctured a lung. They should heal nicely."

All she could do was exhale.

"Now, if you'll move aside, I'll fix him up."

She scooted away and sat with her back to the sofa. She watched the doctor roll Luke to one side and then the other to remove his shirt. It was discarded in a small crumpled pile. Mrs. Brown came forward. She picked up the shirt and gave it to Ada. She assisted Dr. Maxwell while he wrapped Luke's ribs.

Ada clutched Luke's shirt. It smelled of dust and sweat. Luke's sweat. If he would only wake up and forgive her. He had to wake up. If he didn't, she would never forgive herself.

Dr. Maxwell cleaned Luke's cuts and completed his ministrations. Then he stood and helped Ada to her feet.

"Are you feeling well?" He studied her.

"I'll be fine."

He nodded. "I'll return first thing in the morning to see how he is progressing." He patted her arm.

"Thank you."

Mrs. Brown escorted him to the door. The by-standers followed, heads hung low, and shuffled from the room.

Ada remained. The clock ticked so loudly that she had to strain to hear Luke's shallow breathing. She dropped to his side. She grabbed his hand and squeezed it.

"Wake up, Luke. Please, wake up," she murmured.

She scanned his features for any sign of life. She found none except for the slight rise and fall of his chest. She began her vigil.

Chapter Eighteen

"Miss Marsh," Dr. Maxwell began, "it's been three days. I expected Luke to regain consciousness by now." He glanced down at Luke's supine body.

Ada put a hand to her throat in stunned silence.

"I don't want to frighten you, Miss Marsh. The human body is amazingly resilient." His kind eyes offered comfort. "Read to him, and talk to him. That's the best anyone can do."

Dr. Maxwell departed, and she mulled over his words. She would do as the doctor recommended.

She sank to her knees. She picked up Luke's slack hand and held it to her cheek. His color was still ashen. His normally lean frame was gaunt.

She closed her eyes and took a deep breath.

"Luke, I was so senseless. I accepted Lilith's lies when I should have known differently. She told me things that every actress fears. I've even been too close to that situation myself. You'll never know how powerless a woman can feel under the control of a man." She shuddered inwardly. "But I truly believe that *you* are a man of integrity . . . and I hope you will forgive me someday." She wept. "Please wake up, Luke. Please. . . ."

Luke awoke slowly. From the blackness, he could hear Ada's muffled voice. Someone was holding his hand. Was it Ada? His head ached something fierce. It seemed as if someone was sitting on his chest. He was sore. He could tell that without even moving. He felt as if he had been trampled by a herd of horses. No, not a herd, just one. Daisy. He remembered now.

He forced his eyelids open but squinted from the sunlight streaming in the window. He was finally able to focus on a blue wall. He must be at Mrs. Brown's. He rolled his head and observed Ada crying over his hand. His first instinct was to comfort her, but then he recalled their last encounter. He wondered if her tears were for him as one human for another or if she did really care for him. He wouldn't ask her anytime soon. He was still hurt and angry. He had been so consumed by his emotions that he never even saw the trolley coming.

It took a great amount of effort to pull his hand out of hers. He groaned.

Ada's bloodshot eyes snapped open. "Oh, Luke . . . you're awake." Her voice trembled. "How do you feel?" She quickly wiped tears from her cheeks.

"Terrible," he croaked. His throat was parched.

She looked almost as bad as he felt. Her hair had been hastily done up in a lopsided bun. Her clothes were rumpled. It appeared she hadn't slept for days.

"Are you thirsty?" She reached for a glass of water on a nearby table. "You must be. I've tried to give you water and broth, but you have been out for three days."

"Three days?"

"Yes." She held the glass to his lips and wiped his chin with a frilly handkerchief.

"Where's Daisy?"

"Daisy?" She seemed bewildered by his question.

"My horse."

"Oh. Mr. Carey is keeping it down at his livery, free of charge, until you're better."

He nodded slightly. "Was she hurt?"

"As far as I know, she only scraped her forelegs. He thought she would heal just fine."

"Good."

"You've had a concussion and a couple of broken ribs." She spoke tentatively.

He grunted as he attempted to sit up. "I need to get home. The chores—"

She put a firm hand to his shoulder. "We sent word to Mr. Engel. He's taking care of your farm."

"I should still get on home."

"You can't leave. You can't ride your horse like that." She glanced fleetingly at his bandaged torso.

"I'll get Reverend Schneider or someone else to take me home." He knew he sounded gruff. He had to get away from her. He didn't want to see her sympathy. Apparently, she had nursed him for three days. He didn't want to be beholden to her any more than he already was.

"Will you at least wait until Dr. Maxwell returns in the morning?" she asked quietly. She appeared apprehensive and remorseful.

He sighed. He was weak, light-headed, and it was infernally hard to breathe. Maybe after a couple of good meals he would feel more like himself.

"Until mornin'," he agreed.

Her fingers still lingered on his shoulder. They felt cool against his hot skin. She must have realized how intimate the gesture was, because she jerked her hand away.

She reached over to the sofa and retrieved his

shirt. "I cleaned and mended this for you." She looked flustered as she helped him into it. She paused over the buttons.

"I can do it." His voice was curt.

"Of course." She drew back. "We had chicken and noodle soup for lunch. Would you like some?"

He nodded.

She stood and rustled away. She was almost to the door before he spoke. "Ada?" She waited. "Thanks."

Her smile lit up her weary face before she continued out the door.

His heart ached as much as the rest of his body. The betrayal he felt was overwhelming. He just didn't know if he could forgive her or not.

Ada deposited the tray on the kitchen table. The bowl was almost empty. Only a drop of milk remained in the glass. A few crumbs of bread dusted the plate. She was glad Luke's hearty appetite was intact.

She was overcome with thankfulness. She exited the kitchen and quickened her steps. She wanted a chance to apologize to Luke again.

Someone rapped on the front door as Ada passed it. People didn't usually knock at Mrs. Brown's. Curious, she opened it.

Lilith Carlisle was standing on the stoop. She

wore a gaudy off-the-shoulder purple gown that any decent woman wouldn't be seen in during the light of day. She snapped her red silk and gold-fringed parasol shut.

Ada glanced over her shoulder and could see Luke resting peacefully in the parlor. She stepped outside and latched the door behind her.

"I heard Luke had been injured and brought here. You must be a saint to nurse him back to health after all he's done to you." She pretended sympathy.

Ada slowly clapped her hands. "Brava. Such a fine performance, Miss Carlisle." Her voice was thick with sarcasm.

Lilith looked as if she was about to protest but then thought better of it. "So, my game is up, is it?"

"Yes."

"I must say, you were quite a rival. Most women would have given up much sooner." She pushed a wisp of frizzy dark hair away from her powdered face.

Ada's hardened perception of Lilith surprisingly gave way. She was not some ravishing siren. She was a sad woman who painted her face and wore flamboyant garments for attention. She reminded Ada of a scrappy mutt she had encountered outside a hotel in Chicago. It had snarled and barked, but as soon as she stepped toward it, it ran away yelping.

Lilith was like that dog. She made noises and tried to cause trouble, but in the end she was nothing to be afraid of.

"Why did you do all of this to me?" Ada asked.

Lilith apparently wasn't prepared for that question. She opened and closed her mouth a couple of times before she spoke. "I was angry. At first, it was because of your fame, your career, and your handsome fiancé. *I* should have all that." She tossed her head. "But you threw it all away and tried to be self-righteous. Then I saw Luke tripping all over himself for you when he wouldn't give me a second glance. You were no better than me. If I couldn't have him, why should you get him?"

"You might be satisfied after all. I might not get him because of your lies and my stupidity."

Lilith opened her parasol. "Oh, he'll forgive you."

"I hope so. He's been the best thing in my life."

Lilith's eyes told her she agreed, but she didn't admit it out loud. She strolled down the sidewalk. She looked over her shoulder and said, "Tell him I hope he's better soon."

Ada nodded and watched Lilith Carlisle sashay out of her life. They understood each other. She had the feeling they had called a truce.

She inhaled the fresh, albeit hot, air. She hadn't been outside in so long. It felt good, but she had something she must do. It was time to apologize. It was time to tell Luke how she felt about him. He needed to know how much she loved him.

She slipped into the house, went to the parlor, and sat on the floor near him. He looked tired.

"Who was that?" he asked, eyes still shut.

She refrained from brushing the hair from his forehead. "Lilith."

One eye popped open. "What did she want?"

"She sent her regards about your health."

He grunted and closed his eye.

"I think she'll leave us alone now." She thought he cringed at her words.

"I'll believe that when I see it." He paused. "At least you can go back on the circuit to get away from her."

"What?" She couldn't believe her ears. "I'm not going anywhere," she said indignantly.

He raised his shoulders, grimacing from pain. He remained silent.

Her temper flared. So, this was how he wanted to handle the situation? Just send her away so he wouldn't have to deal with her? He had another thing coming.

Several moments passed before she quelled her irritation. She lifted her chin and began, "Luke. We need to talk. You need to know—"

The front door was flung open. Gwen stuck her

head in and looked around. "I'm back!" She waved. She disappeared and returned shortly, dragging her trunk into the entryway. She removed her gloves and hat as she hurried to them.

She plopped down next to Ada. "I came as soon as I could. Walter insisted I go to a function last night for his firm." She put a hand on Luke's sleeve. "Are you hurt badly?"

"I'll live." He smirked.

She turned to Ada. "Thank you for telephoning Walter's office. I hated not being here to help." She appraised Ada. "You look worn out. Have you slept?"

"A little." Ada rubbed her temples.

"Go on up and take a nap. I can sit with him now." She patted her shoulder.

Ada realized how exhausted she was. Maybe she would rest and talk to Luke privately later. She assented and rose. "We'll continue our conversation later," she told him.

His expression was guarded. He didn't respond.

Gwen raised her eyebrows.

Ada gave her a look that promised explanations. "I'll return soon." She turned on her heel and went toward her room for a well-deserved nap.

Chapter Nineteen

Ada never concluded her discussion with Luke. She slept that afternoon and into the night and didn't rise until late the next morning. When she made her way downstairs, he was gone.

Mrs. Brown informed her that he had insisted on returning home. Gwen had found someone to drive them to his farm. She was going to stay with him as long as he needed her.

The only thing Ada could do was wait. She would have to go back to work and bide her time until he was ready to talk.

Luke was laid up in his bed for several more days. Gwen flitted in and out of his room, trying to cheer him. She even asked once what had happened between him and Ada. She dropped the subject in two shakes of a dog's tail at his scowl.

He knew he probably should have stuck it out and had that conversation with Ada, but he just couldn't stomach it. He still couldn't believe she hadn't trusted him. It made him sick. He had been nothing but honorable toward her. Yet she showed her appreciation by accepting the first set of lies hurled her way. And by someone she knew from experience had no morals.

He wasn't sure what he was going to do. All he did know was that it would be a good long while before he wanted to set eyes on her again. And that notion scared him as much as what he might have to say to her.

Ada was in the dress shop with Mrs. Parkinson at the end of the week when the jingling bell over the door disturbed her self-pitying reverie. She was surprised to see Reverend Schneider enter. He removed his hat and came toward her.

She skirted the table and greeted him. "It's good to see you. What brings you here?"

"Miss Dennis asked me to stop by."

"Rose? Are they back so soon? I was under the impression they wouldn't return until autumn."

His kind eyes were grave. "Mrs. Dennis and her daughter have returned with the colonel."

"Oh, good. I'll have to visit them soon."

"I haven't made myself clear, Miss Marsh. They brought the colonel back to bury him. He died from heart failure two nights ago."

"No . . ." she breathed.

"The funeral will be tomorrow morning at ten. Miss Dennis wished that I tell you and Miss Sanders. I'm on my way to her now."

"She's been nursing Luke out at his farm. She's still there."

He nodded. "Thank you. Until tomorrow." He departed quietly.

Poor Rose. The colonel had run his household with military precision. How would she and her mother fare without him?

"Miss Marsh?" Mrs. Parkinson asked.

"Yes, ma'am?"

"It's almost time to close up." She paused from cutting some yellow brocade. "You may leave to offer your condolences to your friend."

"That's so kind of you." She retrieved her hat from under the table and put it on as she dashed to the door. "Thank you."

Ada hurried her steps as she made her way the few blocks to Rose's home. She was breathless by the time it came into view. She slowed her pace and observed several buggies and an automobile in front of the house.

She rang the doorbell. A lady from the church admitted her and showed her to the parlor, where Mrs. Dennis was standing stoically near the fireplace. Sympathetic friends surrounded her.

Ada wound her way through the group and expressed her sorrow to Rose's mother. Mrs. Dennis nodded but had a faraway look about her.

A matronly woman pointed out that Rose was in the back garden. Ada slipped away to find her. She went through the kitchen and peered out the screen door.

In a far corner of the small yard, Rose was sitting on a bench under an arbor covered with white roses. She held a rumpled handkerchief to her face. Her shoulders trembled.

"Oh, Rose . . ." she murmured. She let herself out and went to her friend. "Rose, I'm so sorry," she said.

Startled, Rose looked up. Her eyes and nose were red. Her eyelashes were dewy.

Ada sat next to her and embraced her for a long while.

Rose pulled away and dabbed her eyes. "I appreciate your coming."

"How are you holding up?"

"Fine . . ." She glanced at the house. "I just couldn't stand the pitying looks any longer. I had to get away," she whispered.

"That's understandable." Ada clasped hands with her. "What happened to your father?"

"Mother told me they had just eaten supper and went for a walk along the lake. He complained of indigestion, and before she knew it, he collapsed. . . ." She took a shaky breath. "Some bystanders helped her get him home and into bed. He quit breathing before they could send for a doctor. She sent for me then."

"You weren't in?"

"No." Bitterness was evident in her voice. "They had paired me up with one more gentleman caller. This one was a corporal in the Army. Father seemed particularly pleased with him. We were attending an outdoor concert in the park when I received the news."

"You must have been shocked."

She shook her head. "I was furious. I still am." She crushed the handkerchief. "If they hadn't been so desperate to marry me off . . . I would have been there to say good-bye." She sniffed and held her head high. "Well, I'm having no more of that. I'll not be paraded around before prospective suitors anymore. I'll probably never marry."

"Never?"

Her head drooped. "Well . . . maybe I will. But I'm not going to be in some mad hunt for a husband. If I'm supposed to marry, the right man will come my way."

"That sounds like a reasonable plan." She smiled warmly. "Are you honestly still angry with your parents?"

Rose studied her sadly before answering. "No . . . I'm mad at myself."

"You are? Why?"

Rose spread the damp handkerchief across her knees and tried to smooth out the wrinkles. "I'm sure you could see that my father was a hard man. He wasn't easy to talk to. I gave up trying a long time ago. I'm afraid I wasn't that close to him." She paused. "In the house, people kept coming up to me to comfort me, and I felt like a fraud. I'm afraid my tears were selfishly for me. For what could have been but wasn't." She wagged her head. "I must be the most self-absorbed daughter in the world."

Ada put an arm around Rose's thin shoulders. "I think that's a normal reaction for anyone who loses a parent. We wonder if things could have been better, if we could have been better, closer. And we do mourn for ourselves, the ones left behind."

Rose nodded.

"So grieve for yourself if you need to. Just don't stay in that dark place for long." A revelation came to her about her own life. "Know, too, that you're not alone. My grandmother and other kind people came along when I was in crisis. And, best of all, I found the truest of friends here when I needed them the most. I'll be your confidante whenever you need me." She kissed her cheek.

A timid smile crept across Rose's face. "You're a true friend, Ada." She stood and held out her hand. "And I can face anything with you by my side."

Ada captured Rose's slender hand. Even in this time of sadness, Rose was as sweet and lovely as the flower she was named after.

Ada held a black silk umbrella over Rose and her mother to block the unrelenting sun. The rays seeped into her black serge suit. Sweat trickled down her back.

She was annoyed with herself as her mind wandered again, and her eyes slipped from Reverend Schneider to find Luke. He was standing across the grave from them with the other mourners at Calvary

Cemetery. Gwen was by his side, giving him worried glances from time to time. He was wearing his dark gray church suit. He held his hat in his left hand while he rested his right arm across his ribs. Discomfort was evident on his wan face. It was probably the first time he had been up for an extended period in over a week. She hoped he healed quickly.

Her attention returned to the minister as he offered his final prayer for the colonel and his family. He left his post at the foot of the grave and began the procession of mourners shuffling past Mrs. Dennis and Rose.

Gwen and Luke held back until everyone else was gone. Gwen hurried forward and hugged both women. Luke shook Mrs. Dennis' hand. Reverend Schneider then led Mrs. Dennis toward a black coach.

Luke lingered beside Rose. "I'm so sorry for your loss." His voice was husky.

"Thank you." She appraised him. "Ada told me you had an accident. Are you well?"

"I'm makin' it." Beads of perspiration dotted his upper lip. "But I do believe I've been up long enough for today." He glanced at Gwen and nodded toward his carriage. "Go ahead and get your bags from my buggy, Gwen. If Mrs. Dennis is agreeable, that is, to let her driver take you home."

"Of course we don't mind," Rose offered.

"Are you sure, Luke?" Gwen looked troubled. "I can stay a few more days."

"I'm fine," he said, not convincing anyone. "You don't need to mother me anymore." His eyes landed on Ada but quickly left her face. "I need to be alone a while."

Confusion passed across Gwen and Rose's faces as he tipped his hat and lumbered away. Gwen shrugged and hastened ahead of him to get her bags.

Rose took Ada's arm and whispered, "What happened between you two?"

Ada grimaced as she watched Luke's departing figure. "I was put to a test, and I failed."

"When did all this happen?"

"Right before his accident. I don't know if he'll ever forgive me."

"Why haven't you told me?"

She smiled sadly. "Rose, I came to comfort you, not burden you with my problems."

Rose led her along to meet up with Gwen. "Well, as soon as we get home, you're going to tell us all about it. We'll see what we can do to help."

Ada opened her mouth to protest.

"And we won't take no for an answer."

Ada completed her humiliating story in a silent room. The three women sat on Rose's bed. A slight breeze fluttered the lace curtain.

"Oh, my . . ." Rose said under her breath.

"I can't believe anyone would lie like that—not even Lilith," Gwen fumed.

"I can't believe I accepted her tale without even blinking an eye." Ada shook her head.

Rose patted her hand. "The damage has been done. What do we do now to fix it? Luke is a reasonable man. Surely we can get him to come around."

"I don't know," Gwen sighed. "I've never seen him like this. . . . It's as if the life has gone out of him."

Ada nodded. "There must be something I can do." She put her chin in her hand.

"I could go over there and box his ears to knock some sense into him," Gwen quipped as she stuck out her chest and held her fists up.

"Let's refrain from violence if we can." Ada chuckled.

"I'll talk with him," Rose offered with quiet determination. "I can get him to see reason."

"You'd do that for me? Even with what you're going through?"

"Of course. What kind of friend would I be if I can't give back what's been so generously given to me?"

Ada squeezed her shoulders.

"What's your plan of attack?" Gwen asked.

"I'm not sure yet. But by the time I'm finished, he'll thank me for making him come to his senses."

"I hope so," Ada whispered.

"I will. You just wait and see."

Chapter Twenty

Luke left Dr. Maxwell's office free of his bandages and breathed deeply for the first time in weeks. His side ached some, but his scrapes and cuts had healed into nice pink scars. He was grateful to feel human again.

He warily watched people bustling about. He had been a hermit for the past month. The solitude hadn't helped his attitude any. He wanted to buy his supplies and get back home as soon as possible.

He walked across Main Street to one of the general stores. He entered through the heavy wood-and-glass door. His eyes were adjusting to the dim light when he heard a female voice call his name.

He turned. Rose spoke to her mother and then

came up to him. She was wearing a gray blouse and black skirt for mourning, but she looked good. He was glad to see that grief hadn't worn her down.

"Luke, it's been so long." She scanned him quickly. "How are you?"

"All healed up." He gave her a rusty smile. "How are you and your mother?"

"We're as well as can be expected."

"Good." He nodded.

There was concern in her eyes as she peered up at him.

"Is somethin' wrong?" he asked.

"No. You just . . . seem low. Would you like to join me in a little diversion? It'll do us both good." She was uncharacteristically bold as she put her arm through his. "You owe me a trolley ride. I've been waiting impatiently for you to offer."

He chuckled. It sounded strange after so long. "Miss Dennis, are you free to ride the trolley with me?"

"Why, I'd be happy to." She waved to her mother, and he led her outside.

Before long, Luke had purchased two tickets for a dime and was escorting her to an unoccupied seat at the back of the streetcar. She sat by the window on the edge of the seat. He sat across the aisle from her just before the car lurched forward.

Rose appeared to have something on her mind. He didn't ask her what she wanted to talk about, though. He figured he'd find out sooner or later.

It wasn't until the last passenger had departed and they were alone that she turned to him. "Ada misses you," she said quietly.

He wished she hadn't brought up such a sore subject. He'd been trying for weeks to not ponder over Ada, but she was all he could think about. He still hadn't come up with a solution. He just couldn't forgive her or forget her.

"She's so sorry for what she did."

"She told you?" He was surprised she had admitted her folly.

"Yes." She touched his sleeve. "She's afraid you won't forgive her. She's quite desperate."

"Desperate," he spat out. He shook his head. "Rose, I have been jumpin' through hoops to get that woman to love me. Now, after I find out she never trusted me, she decides she wants me? I'm tired of the whole thing. I'm tired of her."

"Really?"

"Yeah." He rubbed the new scar on his forehead. "She can wallow in her own misery."

Rose was silent a good long while before she spoke. "You will only make yourself unhappy if you don't forgive her."

He swallowed hard. "I just don't know if I can. . . ."

"You're miserable. She's miserable. If you just show a little mercy, you can both be content. You could have such a perfect life. If only . . ."

"If only I'd stop runnin' from her," he murmured.

The trolley stopped, and a few passengers climbed aboard. The last woman was hidden behind a big black hat. He knew, even before he saw her face, that it was Ada.

"Now do you believe it is meant to be?" Rose whispered excitedly.

A chill ran up his spine. He nodded.

Ada's eyes were drawn to them. She was clearly startled to see him. Her fair skin appeared to pale a shade. She made her way to them. She sat across the aisle from him. She was tense, her smile unsure.

The streetcar was moving again before he found his voice. "Ada."

"Luke." She waited for him to continue.

"I think I'm ready to finish that conversation."

Ada settled onto a bench under a young oak tree in Woodland Park. They were away from the commotion of construction of the new library. It took several moments before Luke sat next to her. He removed his hat and put it between them on the bench. He leaned forward, elbows on his knees, and he stared at the ground.

"Thanks for lettin' me take Rose home first."

"Of course. We couldn't just abandon her."

"Nope, we couldn't do that."

She drank in the sight of him. He looked healthy. He had filled out some. His color was good, but the dark smudges under his eyes betrayed the fact that he wasn't sleeping any better than she was.

Silence stretched between them. The speech she had rehearsed over and over for this moment fled. She finally plowed ahead. "Luke, I want you to know how ashamed I am. I'm embarrassed, upset and . . . staggered that I believed Lilith." She wanted to touch his shoulder but refrained. "I'm heartsick. . . . Can you forgive me?"

He bent down and picked up a small twig. It snapped loudly as he broke it into tiny sections. The pieces fell to the ground, one by one.

He exhaled audibly. He continued to stare at his empty fingers as he spoke. "I forgive you, Ada," he paused. "I'm afraid, though, it'll be a while before I can forget."

"I understand." She removed her black gloves and toyed with them while she tried to decide what to say next. "You need to know how much I care for you, Luke. I knew when I saw you on the ground bleeding that I loved—"

"Don't," he said angrily. "Don't say those words now." He shot up off the bench and glared down at her. "Don't you know how long I've waited to hear that? You can't just come to me and tell me like this, after all that's happened."

She stood and put a hand over her mouth. Unwanted tears sprang up. "But I thought you should know," she whispered.

"You think I should know after you ripped my heart out and threw it away?" He stepped toward her.

She clutched her gloves, trying to still her shaking hands. She didn't know how to respond to his anger. She waited, stunned and speechless, knowing she deserved every harsh word.

"You'll never know what I went through because you didn't trust me." He grabbed her shoulders. "I thought I'd die. I thought I'd never get to hold you again, never—"

His hands clasped her face, and he crushed her lips with a kiss. His lips pressed against hers with such force that they were both breathless by the time he pulled away.

"Don't ever do it again." He rested his rough cheek

against hers. His breath was warm as it fluttered against her skin.

"Do what?" Her knees were weak.

"Break my heart."

"I won't," she sighed. "I promise."

He backed away. His dark eyes bored into her. "I'll hold you to that."

She felt pinned like a butterfly. She nodded.

He let go of her. His gaze was downcast. He raked his fingers through his hair. "I think we should start over. Go slower. It might take a long time to rebuild what was lost." He eyed her warily.

"I'll do whatever it takes. However long it takes," she said with conviction.

"Fine." He looked uncomfortable. He motioned for her to take a seat. He soon followed suit. "I apologize for my behavior just now. That was no way to treat a lady." He rubbed the back of his neck.

"You don't need to apologize," she said softly. "You're a passionate man. Never regret being that way." She wanted to add that that was one of the things she loved most about him, but she knew better.

"Thanks." He seemed to be mulling over something. He grunted. "There's just one more thing I want to know, and I'll never bring it up again." He looked at her intently.

"Go on."

"Why did you believe her?"

His voice was so low, she barely heard the question. How many times had she asked herself the same thing? "I know it's no excuse," she began, "but I've seen it so many times before."

"Seen what?"

"Even in this day and age, most men think actresses are no better than harlots. I'm not saying I haven't seen my share of loose women, but more often I have seen men take advantage of these women. They think they can use them and move on without any consequences." She reflected. "I vowed, a long time ago, I would never let that happen to me. I kept up my guard all those years, until I settled here and met you."

"And I hounded you with my 'passionate' personality." He wagged his head.

"I was flattered, but you also scared me a little. I thought I finally trusted you—until Lilith came to me. All the insecurity and contempt I had hidden in my heart rose up and swallowed me." She peeked at him. "That's the only way I know to explain it." She thought she saw a flicker of empathy in his eyes.

He got to his feet. He stood directly in front of her with a wry grin. He bowed formally. "I hear you're the new seamstress in town. I'm tickled Shawnee is growin' enough to need your services. I'm Luke Logan." He extended his hand.

She clasped it and beamed up at him. "I'm Ada Marsh. I'm so glad to meet you." It felt good to smile again. "So glad."

Chapter Twenty-one

"What an evening," Ada mumbled to herself as she let herself into her room, switching the light on as she entered.

She pulled off her black silk gloves and draped them across the bed. She removed her ear bobs and necklace, dropping them onto the dresser. She sighed.

The first evening out with Luke since their reconciliation had been strained. He wasn't angry, but he was still cautious and reserved. Even with Gwen to serve as a buffer between them, he didn't seem to relax during the formal opening of the Carnegie Library. He seemed to admire the two-story brick building with its four marble columns and domed roof. He also appeared impressed by the marble staircase inside the entryway. He was just too quiet. Gwen noticed it also and tried to draw him out with her enthusiasm for the inventory of over a thousand books. He only smiled politely.

The musical program in the small auditorium hadn't boosted his spirits either. The violinist, a Bohemian by the name of Gerald Mraz, had given a superb performance, and later the sweet voice of Miss Carrie McManus touched the hardest heart. With the exception of Luke's, it seemed.

The trio had returned to Mrs. Brown's in a subdued mood. Gwen ran upstairs to write her article about the opening so she could get it into the morning paper. Ada and Luke chatted uncomfortably about trivial matters until Gwen rushed back down and Luke took her to the newspaper office.

Ada was left to herself, wondering if things could ever be the same between them. She was willing to keep trying, though. Maybe their love would be stronger after all of this. At least she hoped so.

Just as she was beginning to unbutton the neck of her plum silk dress, there was a quiet rap on the door.

"It's me," Gwen whispered.

Ada admitted her friend and closed the door softly behind her.

"I just wanted to tell you that Luke didn't know

about the masquerade ball at the end of the month. I told him that it was a fund-raiser for the new church. I told him we were going and that I hope Walter will come down for it. He said he would escort us whether Walter comes or not."

"Not exactly the eagerness I was hoping for," Ada commented.

"He wasn't himself tonight, was he?" Gwen clucked her tongue. "Well, just give him time. He'll come around. He can't hold a grudge for long. It's not in his nature."

"I hope so."

"I'm glad to hear you still have strong feelings for Luke, because I had something else to tell you. I wasn't sure if I should . . ." She wrinkled her brow.

"What is it?"

"I heard tonight, when I went back to the office, that the Hugh Wellington Revue is scheduled to perform in Shawnee soon."

"When?"

"The first of November."

Ada dropped to the bed. Her heart fluttered. She felt her color rise. "I thought I'd never have to see him again."

Gwen sat next to her. "Do you still care for him?"

"No. It's just. . . ." She put a hand to her warm cheek. "He used to have this . . . power . . . over me.

I don't want to see him again. Truthfully, I don't know how I will react to him."

"Oh, Ada." She embraced her. "That means you'll have to see him, or you'll always wonder. You can't let that dangle between you and Luke."

"Even though I don't want to agree," she said after a pause, "I'm afraid you're right. And I dread it with everything that's in me."

He was an idiot. Luke shook his head at himself as he entered his dark house. He set the lantern on the table while he lit an oil lamp. He was an idiot for being in a foul mood all night long. Sure, he couldn't forget what Ada had done, but that was no way to act. He hadn't realized what he had done until he saw the hurt in her eyes when he bid her farewell for the night.

She was sad too. He wasn't the only injured party. She also wasn't some alabaster figurine sitting on a shelf. A shelf, he realized, he had put her on. She was a living, breathing, lovely, complicated woman.

It was time to mend fences. Time to get on with their lives. Together.

"I don't know about this, Gwen." Luke raised an eyebrow as she threw a red velvet cape around his shoulders.

She stepped a few paces back, toward the stove in his parlor. She tapped one temple thoughtfully as she scrutinized him. "You'll be the handsomest man at the ball as Romeo."

"When I asked you to help me think of a costume, this isn't what I had in mind."

"But it's so romantic." She held her hands to her chest and obliged him with a swoon.

"I'm *not* wearin' tights." He glared at her.

"And why not?" she asked.

"If you saw my knees, you wouldn't be askin'."

"So, what was your idea for a costume?"

"A cowpoke."

"I don't think so."

"What's wrong with that?" he asked, tossing the cape onto the couch.

"You look like that all the time."

"Your point is?" He crossed his arms.

"You need to be something different." She paced the floor. "Be adventurous." She stopped in her tracks and snapped her fingers. "That's it. An adventurer, an explorer. Like Stanley and Livingstone." She clapped her hands. "I know what Ada's going as. It'll be perfect."

"Well . . ."

"You have some tall brown hunting boots, don't you?" She headed for his bedroom. "And didn't you wear a pair of tan English riding britches to that fancy hunt in Guthrie a few years ago? You could also wear your hunting vest and a white shirt." She halted.

He almost ran into the back of her. "What?"

"To top it off, I know where I can get one of those straw helmets. Mr. Vance, at the boardinghouse, has one. He wears it when he rides his bicycle." She grinned. "What do you think?"

"Sounds good." He returned the smile. "I'm ready to hunt again."

"Fantastic." She rubbed her chin. "While I'm here . . . I need to borrow some things for *my* costume."

"What's that?"

"You'll see. You'll see."

"Hold still," Ada admonished Gwen as she tied the ribbon.

"I don't like it."

Luke chuckled from his seat on the sofa in Mrs. Brown's parlor.

"I can't stand to have my face covered," Gwen complained. Only her mouth and eyes were visible under the black mask. She untied the ribbon that held it on.

"Then we can make one to hold, like mine." Ada

motioned to the black paper mask next to Luke. Prettily shaped eyeholes were cut out, and it was attached to a short, straight stick that had been painted black.

"No. I'll just wear a bandana."

"A bandana?" Ada asked.

"Sure. That'll be the best."

Ada nodded. "You're right." She picked up her mask and took her place next to Luke. She opened a bottle of glue, dipped a brush in, and began adding small blue and black feathers to her mask.

Gwen sat on the floor and began hemming her costume. "Walter will be so surprised. He would never guess what I'm going to be."

"He won't be too shocked, will he?" Luke asked.

"Walter has as good a sense of humor as anyone. This is all in fun after all."

"When is he gettin' here?" He took a feather from Ada's sack and twirled it between a thumb and forefinger.

"That afternoon." She looked up at him and batted her eyelashes. "I was hoping you would pick him up at the depot, take him to the hotel, and visit with him until we're ready to go to the dance."

"Me? Why me? It's not like we're the fastest of friends."

"Because you're the only person he knows in town. Besides, he likes you. Please?"

He sighed. "All right. We'll have us a rip-roarin' time."

Ada chuckled. "That's one of the things I admire about you."

He smiled and asked, "And what would that be?"

"Your pure, simple generosity," she teased.

He nodded as Gwen laughed at him. "That's me. A right generous soul."

Chapter Twenty-two

"**Y**ou two look wonderful," Rose gushed from atop Ada's bed.

"Are my wings straight?" Ada looked over her shoulder at her blue and black paper butterfly wings. She brushed at the skirt of her peacock blue sateen dress to rid herself of a stray feather.

"Perfect," Rose admired with a wistful smile.

"I wish you could go." Ada squeezed Rose's hand.

"I do too. It just wouldn't be proper." She fingered her black wool skirt. "I'm still in mourning."

"Well, pardner, are you ready to vamoose?" Gwen interrupted in her best cowboy drawl. She wore a

Western hat and pants borrowed from Luke, and a red bandana covered her nose and mouth.

"Yes, sir." Ada curtsied.

Gwen moseyed to the door. Her eyes twinkled as she spoke. "I'll go down first. Why don't you wait on the landing for a moment?"

"I can do that."

Ada and Rose followed Gwen, but they paused as she'd asked. Gwen soon disappeared down the stairs. They could hear Luke laugh in surprise. Walter was silent.

A moment passed before Gwen asked, "What do you think, Walter?"

"It's amusing, Gwendolyn. Now, go put on your real costume." His tone of voice bordered on contempt.

Ada and Rose exchanged wide-eyed glances.

"But—"

"You cannot appear in public with your limbs showing in that manner."

"Yes, Walter," Gwen said softly.

She trudged up the stairs. She untied the bandana and yanked off the hat. "I wasn't sure I liked it anyway," she told them.

"What are you going to do?" Rose patted her shoulder.

"Let's go through my trunk of costumes. We can find something." Ada hurried to a large trunk in a corner of her room. She opened it and motioned them over to look. They began to rummage through it.

"I'll never be able to wear any of these tiny things," Gwen said with disgust.

"Keep looking. Maybe there's something we can make do with," Ada encouraged.

"Oh, look at this." Rose pulled out a midnight taffeta gown. Tiny jet beads dotted the dress. Small, downy black feathers encircled the low neckline, cap sleeves, and hem. She stood and held it up to her. "It's the most beautiful gown I've ever seen," she breathed.

"You would look beautiful in it," Gwen offered.

"It looks like it would fit," Ada observed with a practiced eye. "Won't you come with us, Rose? You'll be in mourning colors."

"I couldn't."

"There is an extra mask. Gwen didn't want to use it, but I finished it off with black feathers on a whim. It would cover almost your entire face. You probably wouldn't even be recognized."

"I don't know. . . ." She looked tempted. "What could I be?"

There was silence until Ada rushed to her bed and felt around underneath it. She pulled out another pair of black wings with feathers around the edges. "A swan. A black swan." She held them up triumphantly. "I started these, but I didn't think they were big enough. They'll be perfect for you."

"I really shouldn't."

"I have some black ostrich feathers for your hair."

Gwen peered up from amid the colorful garments. "You'll be the mysterious beauty of the ball."

"Me? Mysterious?"

"Come with us." Ada tried to contain her excitement.

Rose considered carefully. She nodded and soon beamed.

"Wonderful." Ada came forward. "I'll help you change."

"What in the world are these?" Gwen broke in. She held up a pair of green and white striped stockings.

Ada chuckled. "Those go with an Irish lass costume. That bright green wool skirt goes with it."

"Irish lass?" she mused. "I've always been fascinated by Ireland."

She got to her feet and stepped into the full skirt. It lacked a good three inches before it would fasten at her waist. It was so short, it hit her around the shins. "It won't work," she sighed.

"Yes, it will. They wore them short to show their

stockings. It's not indecent by any means." Ada reached over and tugged at the waistband. "I can add an extension in no time at all. We can put a big bow back here to hide it. You could take your hair down and put on a matching bow."

"What would I do for a bodice?"

"Don't you have a green and red plaid vest?"

She nodded.

"Wear that over your linen nightgown with the scooped neck and loose sleeves. No one will be able to tell what it is."

"Perfect!" she exclaimed.

"You and Rose help each other to change. I'll work on this." She helped Gwen out of the skirt and hastened to her sewing box.

"I'll telephone Mother first and tell her I'm going to spend the night here," Rose added before they left the room.

It was no use trying to talk to Walter anymore. Luke had made an effort to chat with him for Gwen's sake, but when Walter sent her upstairs, he didn't see any reason to put himself out any longer.

He lounged back on the sofa, his hands behind his head, his legs crossed at the ankles. He appraised Walter, who was pacing impatiently in front of the fireplace. The man wore a top hat and tails and a sash with the word MAYOR written across it in bold letters.

No nonsense. No banter. No fun. That seemed to sum up Walter Manning. He wondered what Gwen saw in him. There must be some quality that was hidden from general view. Well hidden.

The minutes ticked on. He was more than relieved when he heard footsteps and loud whispers at the top of the stairs.

He got to his feet and waited in the foyer. Walter was slow to join him. They were looking up as one of the girls descended elegantly in a black dress with wings. The blond hair secured under big black feathers gave her away.

"Rose." Luke held his hand out to her and helped her down the last step. "Just beautiful. You're as graceful as a swan." He snapped his fingers. "A swan. I figured it out, didn't I?"

"Yes." She flashed him a nervous smile underneath her mask.

"I'm glad you're coming with us." He winked at her.

His attention was quickly diverted when he heard light footsteps on the stair treads. He was entranced by Ada. His Ada. She nearly floated down to him. How could she be more exquisite each time he saw her?

She pirouetted for him. She dropped her mask, eyes twinkling.

"Now I know why Gwen insisted I carry that huge net on a stick instead of a gun. It's better to catch you with a butterfly net." He held out his arms and encircled her. He put his lips to her ear and whispered, "You can bet I won't let you go." He felt gooseflesh on her arms.

"And be assured, I won't flit away," she breathed.

Walter cleared his throat loudly and scowled at their public display of affection. Luke resigned himself to being a gentleman and extracted himself from Ada.

"Are you ready, Gwendolyn?" Walter called up the empty stairway.

"Coming!" Gwen appeared at the top of the stairs, straightening the green bow in her flowing hair. She rushed down in a flash of color.

Luke chuckled. Ada and Rose smiled.

Walter inspected her from head to toe. "And you are . . ."

"An Irish lass," she informed him in her best Irish brogue. She dimpled and curtsied for him.

"I suppose that's better than the other." He turned toward the front door. "At least we're not in Guthrie," he muttered as he walked past Luke.

"What was that, Walter?" Gwen asked, trying not to look hurt by his reaction.

"Nothing, my dear." He smiled as he paused at the door. "We're abominably late. Let's go." He held out a hand.

"Yes, Walter." She lifted her wrap off the hall tree.

Luke squeezed her shoulders as she came by. "You look great, lassie."

She gave him an appreciative glance before she hurried to her betrothed.

He wanted to thrash Walter for being such an egotistical dolt. As soon as he got the chance, he wanted to strongly suggest to Gwen that she cast Walter aside before it was too late.

"Let's be on our way, lad and lasses," Gwen said, her enthusiasm and brogue intact. "It's starvin', I am."

Chapter Twenty-three

The group was in a jovial mood. They walked off the elevator to the ballroom on the fifth floor of the Norwood Hotel. They entered the large, sparkling room. Skylights in the ceiling were black chasms to glittering stars. Tremendous chandeliers gave a golden glow to the autumnal decorations. Dried cornstalks as well as pumpkins and gourds were arranged in each corner. A long lace-covered table against one wall was laden with punch and pastries. A string quartet was playing at one end of the room for the brightly costumed dancers.

Ada beamed up at Luke.

He grinned at her, handed his net to Walter, and bowed to her. "May I have the pleasure?"

"I'd be delighted, dear sir." She took his hand, and he whisked her away.

Their quick steps matched the cadence of the lively polka. She felt as light as air under his lead.

"You're quite a dancer, Mr. Logan."

"You can thank my mother and Gwen for that." He paused while he twirled her. "I never thought all those dance lessons with Gwen would pay off so well."

She laughed and was going to tease him about practicing with his younger cousin when he faltered and stopped in his tracks. Another young couple barely missed colliding with them.

"What in the world?" she asked.

He was glaring across the room. She followed his gaze. She gasped as she recognized Hugh in his Hamlet costume. He was standing arrogantly in the entryway. He swept into the room, his royal blue cape fluttering in his wake.

"Don't worry, Ada. I won't let him near you," Luke assured her.

"Thank . . . you." She thought that was what she wanted. She tore her eyes from Hugh and found Luke studying her. "Thank you," she repeated. She gave him what she hoped was a confident smile before they took off again.

* * *

"Luke, I must catch my breath," Ada puffed. Her forehead glistened with moisture.

"I'm sorry, darlin'." He stopped and steered her aside. He glanced over his shoulder and saw Hugh dancing with Lilith, who was dressed up as Cleopatra. "I've been tryin' to keep an eye on that snake."

"I understand."

"I don't know why he had to turn up again," he fumed.

"Gwen said he and his players are going to perform here next week."

"You knew he was comin'?"

"Yes," she said quietly.

"Why didn't you tell me?"

"I didn't think it was important."

"Not important?" he whispered harshly. He looked around to see if anyone overheard. "Don't you think I'd like to know that your former fiancé was going to be in town?" He despised the jealousy that was surfacing. It made him feel pitiful and weak.

She appeared startled by his harsh tone. Her eyes were wide. She bit her trembling lower lip.

"Oh, darlin'," he sighed. He caressed her cheek. "Forgive me for bein' a green-eyed idiot?"

Relief flooded her face. "Of course."

He smiled sheepishly and took her elbow. They

walked toward Gwen and Walter, who were holding glasses of punch by an open window. The cool breeze was refreshing. Luke removed his helmet and fanned his warm face.

"You two don't look like you've broken a sweat. Haven't you been out there?" Luke nodded to the dance floor.

"A time or two." Gwen sampled her drink. "Walter has a bad knee."

"I do believe I've rested enough." Walter suddenly joined the conversation. "Would you care to join me, Miss Marsh?"

She nodded and smiled at Luke over her shoulder as they began to walk forward.

"I hope you know, Manning, you're the only one I trust her with. I've had to fight men off all evenin'," he called after them.

"I'll take excellent care of her, Logan." There was a suspicious gleam in Walter's eye as he led Ada away.

Luke watched them dance. "He's holding her far too close."

"Oh, don't be ridiculous. Walter is a perfect gentleman," Gwen told him.

"A gentleman? So, is that why you're marryin' that piece of dry toast?"

"How rude." Her dander came up as she faced him.

"I'm serious. I'd like to know," he said sincerely. "Why are you goin' to marry him?"

"Because he asked." She shrugged. "Mother says he's good for me. He's a solid tether for someone like me, whose head is always in the clouds."

"Ah, Gwen. What about someone to fly in those clouds with you?"

She was taken aback. He could tell she had never even considered such a thing.

"Just think about it?" He nudged her. "Whatever you decide, you know I'm always around for you."

"Thank you."

"So . . . where's Rose?" he asked, trying to lighten the mood.

She pointed to the dancers nearby. "She's danced with him a few times this evening."

The young man wore a nice brown suit and a store-bought lion mask. His wavy blond hair was combed back. He was politely smiling at Rose. She seemed mesmerized by him.

"Who is that fella?" he asked, protective urges rising.

"I didn't recognize him, but I've seen him talk with Mr. and Mrs. Burke and another man."

"Humph. Doesn't look like I'm goin' to get any rest tonight for lookin' after my girls." He crossed his arms.

"I believe your girls can look after themselves."
She elbowed him.

"So you say," he mumbled as Walter made his
way toward them. Alone. "Where's Ada?"

"Some man in tights cut in." He looked as if
someone had ruffled his feathers. "He was quite in-
sistent."

"Wellington." Luke spat out the name. He scanned
the crowded room. He couldn't spot them. He stepped
forward.

"Luke . . ." Gwen said.

He paused.

"Just . . . think before you leap."

He gave her a curt nod. "I'll be back."

"Where are you taking me, Hugh?" Ada asked,
trying to remove her elbow from his grip.

The elevator doors opened, and he guided her to
the second floor.

"To the balcony, of course. You said you desired
fresh air."

The balcony. That should be safe enough, she reasoned. It was in full view at the front of the building.

He opened the French doors and motioned for her
to step through the archway onto the small platform.
A startled couple excused themselves, leaving Ada
alone with Hugh.

"It is a lovely evening, is it not?" he asked, stroking his mustache.

"It was." She eyed him suspiciously. "Why have you really commandeered me?"

"Always one to get right to the point." His accent sounded clipped and harsh to her ears.

"I have to, around you." She remembered his assertive nature all too well. She seemed to get herself into precarious positions when he used his powers of persuasion.

"My dear Ada." He held his hands up and moved toward her.

She shifted back warily.

He drew himself up and appeared injured. "I returned to this frontier village to confess my sentiments to you. I miss you, my jewel. The troupe misses you. I would be overjoyed if you would be my companion again. Rejoin the company," he urged.

"I'm not interested."

"You've pierced my heart." He put a hand to the supposedly offended area. "We need you. I need you. Not only personally, but, well . . . the troupe is having financial difficulties. We need your instruction, or the company you worked so laboriously to build will crumble."

"You need money." She smirked. "That's the only reason you've come back, isn't it?"

"Rubbish." He grabbed her roughly. "I have yearned for you for an eternity. I want you back."

"Hugh, I—"

"Give me one more chance. I'll see that you are well satisfied. Let me be your lover."

He seized her face before she could speak. His mouth enveloped hers with skillful execution. His mustache prickled her skin. He all but smothered her. He released her with a triumphant light in his eyes.

She wanted to be angry, but all she could do was grin. He repulsed her, and her heart sang. He no longer had any control over her. She was Luke's and his only.

"Valiant effort, Hugh," she said in high spirits. "Good-bye." She walked to the door. She stopped and watched him struggle for composure. "And don't bother to ever come back."

Luke arrived at the French doors just in time to hear that actor ask to be Ada's lover. His heart jumped to his throat. It ached so much, he could say nothing as Hugh put his hands on her and kissed her.

He was about to rush out there and bash him once and for all when Ada smiled. She smiled at the man. How could she? After all they had been through, how could she?

He spun around and ran. He ran like the coward he was. He'd told her not to break his heart, but she didn't listen.

He thought he heard someone call his name, but he ignored it. He clattered down the stairs. He paused halfway down. He had told her he wouldn't let her go. Was he going to give up that easily? Hugh Wellington wasn't any more of a man than he was. He marched back up.

"Blazes, if I'll let him have her! He's got another thing comin'!"

Chapter Twenty-four

Ada was sure she saw Luke disappear around the corner. She cried out his name. There was no response. She picked up her skirts and dashed after him. She didn't know what he'd seen, but she knew she had some explaining to do.

She found him on the landing at the top of the stairs. He looked furious. It was all or nothing. She flung herself into his arms. He grasped her to keep them both from falling, but he quickly put her aside.

"Luke, I don't know how much you saw—"

"I saw and heard plenty," he said through gritted teeth. "He asked to be your . . . lover . . . and you kissed him."

"*He* kissed me."

"You gave him a big ol' grin afterward. You . . . you . . ." he sputtered.

"Did you stay long enough to hear me tell him good-bye?"

He reluctantly shook his head.

"So you didn't hear me tell him to never come back?"

"No . . ."

"Lucas Logan, you mean to tell me you thought I was kissing him and smiling at him because I still care for him?" She put her hands on her hips. Her ire was up now.

He remained stony and silent.

"I learned to trust you. I thought you trusted me." She glared at him.

He seemed to squirm a mite.

"I wasn't smiling about him. I realized when he was drooling all over me that I have absolutely no feelings for him. It's you I love, you big oaf!" She jabbed his shoulder with her index finger.

Hope and then relief played over his handsome features. "Honestly?"

"Yes, Luke." She spread her fingers across his sturdy chest. She wanted to lay her cheek there and feel his strength for the rest of her life.

"Oh, Ada," he sighed. "I'm sorry." He pulled her close. "I love you so much."

She tipped her head back and gazed into his dark eyes. "I love you, Luke. I think I always have. I just didn't know it."

The corners of his mouth turned up. "I told you that you would see it my way someday."

"Yes, you did," she agreed.

She stood on tiptoe and kissed him soundly. He gathered her to him and returned her kiss eagerly. They stumbled. He caught her and pressed her against the wall, crushing her wings. He finally wrenched himself away from her. There was no mistaking the intense flame smoldering in his eyes. Her heart raced.

He stepped back and took a shaky breath. He ran a hand down her left arm and stopped when his lean fingers touched hers. He brought them to his lips.

"We should go back to the party," he murmured.

She had never felt more cherished. She had never known such an honorable man. He cared enough to not make any lewd suggestions. These weren't indecent emotions they felt for each other. She finally knew what honest love was.

He was a big clod. Luke shook his head as they lumbered up the stairs to the ballroom. Why Ada still loved him was beyond him. From then on he was going to count his blessings and be thankful, not jealous or rash in his judgments. He had learned some valuable lessons lately. He never wanted to forget them.

Ada giggled. "What are you thinking about?"

"Just realizing how stupid it would have been for me to run away again."

They paused outside the doors of the ballroom.

"I'm glad you came back to fight for us." Light streamed out of the room, turning her eyes into twinkling emeralds.

"So am I." He fingered one of her wings. "It's a little bent, but do you think you can still fly across the dance floor with me?"

"Of course."

He took her into his arms, and they floated to the music. He had wasted most of the evening. He was finally able to relax and enjoy Ada's company.

He took Gwen out for a turn or two. He tried not to grumble when other men danced with Ada. He knew she only had eyes for him.

He even snagged a chance to dance with Rose. The fellow who had captured most of her attention that evening seemed to have vanished. There was a lighthearted air about her. He was pleased she had decided to come.

"So, who is this mystery man who's taken up your

time this evenin'?" he asked. He knew she was blushing under her mask.

"I don't know." She smiled ruefully. "I was being silly. I was trying to be mysterious and not let him know who I was. But he had to leave before we introduced ourselves."

"Really?"

"A man came with a telegram. It must have been terrible news. He was really shaken by it. He said he had to go back to Wichita immediately."

"He didn't say if he would return?"

She shook her head. She seemed to be struggling for words. She finally peered up at him. "I was hoping to get to know him."

He cleared his throat, trying to decide how to comfort her. "If he is the right one, he'll be back."

She was encouraged a little, but the light had gone out of her eyes.

"Are you ready to leave?" he asked.

"Yes."

"Let's gather the others and go on home."

They found Ada and Gwen chatting with a couple of young men, who excused themselves rather quickly when they arrived.

"Who set a fire under them?" Luke asked as they scurried away.

Gwen snickered. "I'm sure it had nothing to do with your menacing scowl."

"Who, me? I'm a pussycat."

All three women laughed at him.

He pretended to be miffed. "Just for that, I'm takin' you home." He surveyed the room. "Where's Walter?"

"He's leaving early in the morning. He just went down to his room," Gwen explained as they collected their things.

It wasn't long before they arrived at the boardinghouse in Luke's buggy. Gwen and Rose were kind enough to desert them and hurry inside.

Luke jumped down and assisted Ada to the ground.

"It was quite a night." He wagged his head. "Although there are some things about it I'd like to forget."

"But there are so many other things to remember." Her face was radiance and shadows in the glow of the gas streetlights. Her eyes gleamed with affection.

"I do recall some lovely lady telling me she loves me." He tapped his chin.

"I believe that's true." She smiled up at him.

"I'm tickled to hear it. Maybe she'll tell me again?"

"Maybe," she flirted.

He encircled her with his arms. "I've never seen so many men ask a woman to dance as happened to you tonight." He kissed her temple, then the silky spot next to her eye.

"I'm just the current entertainment," she whispered. "It will ebb."

"My love for you will never fade."

"Nor mine for you."

His lips found her neck. He nibbled his way up to her ear. She shivered. Was it from the cool night air or from him?

" 'How do I love thee? Let me count the ways,' " she quoted. "I love your wit, your trust in God, the way your dark eyes sparkle when you look at me, and . . ." she murmured, turning her face to kiss him.

If she was trying to distract him, it worked. But he was more than curious to hear what she had to say. He paused from their activities and prompted softly, "And?" He leaned back to see her better.

She opened her enchanting eyes and studied him. "Your fine physique, even your scars—old and new—and those lips . . . which lead me to your kisses. . . ."

Any shred of resentment he harbored toward her melted away as their lips touched. He wanted her to be his wife. He didn't know when he would ask, but he knew it would be soon.

Chapter Twenty-five

November's weather was mild. The trees began to turn to rust, gold, and burgundy. The town was bustling with anticipation of the upcoming holidays.

Ada and Gwen were both required to work the day after Thanksgiving. Luke, Gwen, and Ada decided not to travel to Guthrie for the big Thanksgiving dinner but to have a tranquil day at his house. Rose's mother was not up to celebrating the day, yet she did encourage her daughter to join her friends.

On the eve of Thanksgiving, Ada, Gwen, and Rose were busy baking pies in Mrs. Brown's kitchen. That is, Gwen and Rose were trying to teach Ada how to bake.

"I think there's more flour on me than in this

crust," Ada moaned as she paused from rolling the dough.

Rose giggled and picked up Ada's crust. "Now we fold it over and place it in the pie tin," she instructed. "Unfold it carefully, and roll the edges under, and pinch them like this." She demonstrated.

Ada tried her hand at it. The result was uneven and crooked. "It looks pitiful."

"Don't worry. It will get easier the more you practice." Rose attempted to repair the damage.

"Believe me, it will still taste wonderful, and Luke won't give a hoot what it looks like," Gwen added. She stirred a gooey concoction that would somehow become the filling for the pecan pie. She poured it into the prepared crust and placed pecan halves on top. "The pecans from Luke's trees are tasty this year." She popped one into her mouth.

"The steamed pumpkin is cool enough to strain now," Rose commented as she pushed globs of orange pulp through a sieve with a spoon.

Ada worked at rolling out another crust. This attempt was easier than the last but still left her frustrated. "You two must always live nearby. Luke will dry up and blow away if I ever have to cook for him."

"You'll learn." Gwen patted her shoulder. "Since he hasn't expired from his own cooking, I believe he'll do just fine with yours."

"If you say so."

"I do. Now, let's peel those apples."

Early the next morning, Luke chauffeured his three favorite women to his home. Each held a basket full of jars, pies, and bread. They attacked his kitchen with a vengeance. Gwen opened the oven and nodded with approval at the wild turkey he had killed, dressed, and put in to bake per her instructions. Before long, great smells wafted through the house.

Luke did his morning chores, cleaned up, and couldn't resist lounging at the table to watch the activity. More precisely, though, he admired Ada. She was as fetching as always. She wore the lavender shirtwaist she had been wearing when they first met. She had mended the torn sleeve and extended the black lace on the cuffs to cover the repair. Not only was she beautiful, but she was skilled as well.

She caught him regarding her and returned the gesture until the pot of potatoes boiled over. When that situation was resolved, she frowned and shook a finger at him. She apparently wasn't going to dally with him anymore until after dinner. He could wait.

"That was an incredible meal, ladies." Luke scooted his chair back and patted his stomach.

"Even my efforts were edible," Ada agreed.

"I believe I'd keep you around even if you couldn't cook a thing. You're pretty handy to have about." He fingered the sleeve of her shirtwaist.

Ada smiled, remembering the day they'd met. Luke had swept her off her feet—literally.

Gwen looked down her nose at them. "There are other ladies present. Can you refrain from such adoration in front of us?"

"Maybe." He grinned.

"Good. We'll clean up this mess, so we can have the rest of the afternoon free."

"Sounds good to me," he assented.

They rose to their feet and began clearing away the dishes. Luke vanished into another room. Ada was pouring a hot kettle of water into the sink basin when he returned. He came up behind her, removed the kettle from her possession, placed it on the stove, and steered her toward the door.

"Just what do you think you're doing?" Gwen furrowed her brow.

"Goin' outside to admire Ada in peace and quiet."

"Fine." She waved them away, trying not to smile.

Luke let them out. He placed Ada's hand in the crook of his arm. They strolled down one of the many paths into the woods. Dried leaves crunched underfoot. The air was cool, but a wrap wasn't necessary.

They passed the barn and made their way up a small incline. They stopped in the middle of a meadow at the top of a knoll. They looked back at the fields, trees, and house with its outbuildings.

"How lovely," she told him.

"Thank you."

"It's . . . it's like the home I was afraid to dream of." She took in the simple beauty.

"You don't know how good it does my heart to hear you say that." He turned to face her. His expression was serious. "Ada, I know I told you that I would need time . . . to go slower, but. . . ." His eyes searched hers. "I just can't wait. Ada, will you marry me?"

She hadn't expected a proposal. She was thrilled speechless.

"I want to give you this before you answer." He dug into a trouser pocket. He pulled out something gold and shiny. He held her hand tenderly and placed a ring on her finger.

It was a slender band with a raised heart and fili-greed ornamentation. An oval diamond shimmered from the center and was surrounded by five small emeralds.

"Oh, Luke," she gasped. "It's lovely."

"I wanted to buy one with emeralds, to match your eyes. When I saw this ring, I knew it was the one."

"It's too expensive."

"I was able to swing it."

She held her hand up and admired the exquisite workmanship.

"Ada? I'm dyin' here, waitin' for your answer."

She focused back on his handsome, albeit worried, face.

"Would you spend the rest of your life by my side? I'll never be a rich man, but you'll always have a safe place to lay your head. You and our children would never want for anything. Will you, Ada? Will you be my wife?"

She knew she must have been grinning from ear to ear as she threw herself into his waiting arms. "I thought you'd never ask." She smothered him with kisses. She savored the softness of his neck, the stubble on his chin, the warmth of his eager lips. Several long moments passed before they separated themselves.

"I'm on top of the world," he murmured.

"I'm the one who is blessed." She shook her head. "I'm in awe." She ran her fingers along the line of his jaw.

"I am too." He captured her hand and kissed her palm.

Gooseflesh ran up her spine.

"I know you'll want to do the wedding up right.

I'll wait as long as you want." His lips trailed to her wrist.

"I don't need a fancy ceremony. I don't want to wait long."

"I was hopin' you'd say that." He grasped both her hands in his. "When?"

She considered it. "Christmas. What better way to celebrate the birth of our life together than on that day?"

"An entire year? I don't know—"

"Not a year from now. *This* Christmas." She squeezed his hands.

"That sounds wonderful."

"And you'll always be able to remember our anniversary," she teased.

He took her into his arms again and gave her a quick kiss on the top of her head. "Believe me, I'll never forget the most joyful day of my life."

Chapter Twenty-six

The next few weeks blurred into a flurry of activity. So much so that Ada had no time to contemplate the rumor that Lilith Carlisle had left town for good. She received a letter from Lisette around that same time and was glad to hear from her former employee. Lisette told her the troupe was making their way, although sales were not quite what they had been when Ada was with them. She also wrote that Lilith Carlisle had joined up with them in Oklahoma City, and she insinuated that Lilith was aligning herself with Hugh. So be it. None of it mattered one whit to Ada. That was her old life. She was getting married.

She tendered her resignation to Mrs. Parkinson,

explaining that it wouldn't be feasible for her to travel back and forth to town from Luke's farm every day. Her employer was sad to see her go, but she bestowed upon Ada a wedding gift of yards of white silk veiling with scalloped edges.

Mrs. Parkinson also offered to assist Ada with her gown. Ada already knew she owned the perfect gown. She wanted to wear the white lace dress Luke had admired, even though it was a summer dress. With Mrs. Parkinson's assistance, they made a long, fitted coat of white velvet and lace to remedy the problem. It contained a single pearl button at the waist to expose the dress underneath. Ada was proud of the finished product.

Christmas Eve was a bustling day. Ada spent the morning packing her trunks with everything she wouldn't need for her wedding. Luke arrived just before noon, and she helped him load her things onto his old farm wagon.

The sky was gray, and there was a nip in the air, but Ada snuggled next to Luke for the ride to his house and wasn't uncomfortable at all. Her spirits were high as they pulled up to Luke's home. It was difficult to imagine that by this time the next day it would be her home also.

Luke's entire family was in town for the wedding.

Some were in their rooms at the Norwood, and his parents were staying at his house. When she and Luke let themselves into the warm kitchen, Luke's mother turned from the stove and stopped stirring whatever was in the big pot. His father was sitting at the table and lowered the newspaper he'd been reading.

"How are you today, my dear?" Mrs. Logan asked as she wiped her hands on her apron.

"Wonderful." Ada grinned.

Mrs. Logan gave her a knowing smile as she informed them, "You're just in time. The brown beans and fried potatoes are done, and I was about to take the cornbread out of the oven."

"Sounds terrific." Luke rubbed his hands together in anticipation. "Could you help me carry Ada's trunks in before we eat, Pa?"

"Surely." He folded the paper and followed Luke outside.

Ada took off her coat, hat, and gloves and hung them on the coatrack off the parlor. She returned to the kitchen to assist Mrs. Logan. Ada placed plates and silverware on the table as Mrs. Logan ladled steaming beans into a serving bowl. Ada scooped the potatoes out of a cast iron skillet onto a large platter while her soon-to-be mother-in-law cut up the cornbread and put it on a plate.

Everything was ready by the time the men were finished. They all sat together at the table. Ada knew that, to the Logans, this was just another meal, but to her it was the first time in many years that she felt like part of a family.

Ada didn't know how such simple fare could be so delicious. She would have to ask Mrs. Logan about it.

She had her opportunity while they were cleaning up, and she made careful mental notes of Mrs. Logan's instructions.

Ada had just put the last plate into the cupboard when Luke emerged with a menacing-looking handsaw.

"May I be of assistance?" Ada asked playfully.

"Yes. We're going to go get our first Christmas tree."

A warm glow spread through her at the thought. How long had it been since she'd had a Christmas tree? She hurriedly donned her outdoor things and joined him on the porch.

He took her gloved hand and led her into the woods. He whistled a carol as they searched for the best tree. They finally came to a stand of fragrant cedars.

"How about this one?" Luke asked. He stood next to it. It was about a head taller than he and flawless.

"Perfect." She clapped her hands with glee. "We'll pop some corn and string it. I'm sure I have some red ribbon in my trunk to make bows. . . ." Her mind raced with ideas on how to decorate the tree.

"And I have a tin star to put on top." He smiled.

He dropped his saw, embraced her, and twirled around before placing her back on the ground.

"I'm so happy," he whispered against her ear.

"So am I, Luke." Tears sprang into her eyes. "You have no idea how very happy I am."

Christmas morning arrived cold and blustery, yet clear skies promised a superb day.

Gwen and Rose assisted Ada as she prepared for the ceremony. She donned her lace gown and over-coat. Her hair was piled up with extra curls. The knee-length veil was securely attached to her hair, along with a wreath of white fabric orange blossoms.

She noted the time, put on her long wool cape, and picked up her bouquet. She had made her own arrangement with cedar from the trees at Luke's place, ivy from a pot in Rose's bedroom, a few white silk roses, and white bows. Streamers of white ribbon cascaded down the front.

"Is everyone ready?" Ada asked.

"Yes," they chorused.

They made the brisk walk to the small, picturesque, clapboard church. Cedar boughs with white velvet ribbons arched over the doors. They paused in the small vestibule to remove their outer garments. Rose went ahead and prepared to sing.

Ada peered around Gwen and was touched to see the church packed with Luke's family and their friends.

"Are you nervous?" Gwen whispered into her ear.

"No. I've never felt more secure." She smiled at her good friend.

"Welcome to the family." Gwen embraced her. "I hope you and Luke have unending happiness." She kissed her cheek.

"Thank you."

A tear sprang up in Ada's eye as Rose's lilting voice filled the church with strains of "O Holy Night". Ada hoped she would always remember the beauty and tenderness she felt at this instant.

When Rose concluded the carol, the organist began the wedding march. Luke was standing in front with his brother, Peter, at his side. Luke turned expectantly. He was so handsome, wearing a gray morning suit with white tie. He appeared awestruck when he spotted her. He placed a hand over his heart. Love beamed from his eyes.

Gwen walked down the center aisle. Ada stepped forward to begin her future. To become Luke's wife.

"Mrs. Brown has outdone herself." Luke whistled low as he surveyed the table groaning with food.

"Yes," Ada agreed, taking her eyes off her husband for only a moment.

The wedding breakfast buffet was a sumptuous mix. Roasted beef and chicken, dainty crustless sandwiches, cookies, a chocolate cake, and candies were spread out across the table. In the center was a two-tiered spice cake decorated with white icing and a circle of fabric orange blossoms.

Family and well-wishers gathered around to congratulate them.

Rose came to them and gave them each a peck on the cheek. "I'm so happy for you two." She squeezed Ada's hand. "Many blessings for you."

"For you too." Ada leaned to her ear. "Next year will be *your* year."

Rose blushed and said, "I don't know about that."

"I just have a feeling." Ada hugged her. "Make sure you take a piece of the cake home and put it under your pillow tonight. You'll dream of your true love."

"That's a bunch of nonsense."

"If you do it, I'd wager a flaxen-haired man will fill your dreams."

"I'll let you know." Rose's mouth turned up. She blushed as she moved away.

"Attention! Attention!" Peter raised his glass of punch. "It's time for a toast." Everyone raised his or her goblet. "To my little brother and his enchanting bride. I'll never know how he won her over—"

"He carried on 'til she plum tuckered out!" someone shouted.

The crowd tittered happily.

"That's my guess." Peter nodded. His countenance quickly sobered. "May the two of you love each other well."

"Hear! Hear!" they all agreed.

Ada tilted her head back and smiled at her husband.

He brushed his lips against hers.

"That's enough of that, Lucas." His mother interrupted them by tapping him on the shoulder. She gave them a warm smile and embraced them. "I'm so glad you've joined this rowdy bunch, Ada. Perhaps all hope of civilizing them isn't lost."

"I wouldn't count on it, Mother."

"Even so, welcome, Ada. You and Enid are the daughters I never had. I'm so proud."

"And I'm so grateful." Ada's eyes misted. "To finally have a family of my own."

"We'll always be here for you, dear." She patted her hand. "Now, let's get you two some food. You're both entirely too thin."

Ada and Luke ate their fill. They enjoyed the company of their relatives and friends. All joined in when Rose and Gwen began singing Christmas carols.

Sometime later Luke rested his hand on the small of her back. "Are you ready to go?"

She nodded, and they made their way through the crowded room. They said their farewells. Everyone flocked after them and waved as they hurried to their buggy.

She snuggled under an ivory and green wedding-ring quilt Luke's mother had given them for a present. She looked back one last time as he drove them away.

They had journeyed only a few blocks when he pulled over to the side of the road.

"Did we forget something?" she asked.

"Just this." He leaned to her and kissed her soundly. "I've been waitin' all day to do that, Mrs. Logan."

"So have I, Mr. Logan." She pressed her cold lips

to his again. "It was a wonderful day, wasn't it?" she murmured.

"It sure was." His eyes clouded. "Although, I am sorry there's no grand wedding tour for you. Maybe in the spring . . ."

She placed her gloved hands on either side of his strong, sensitive face. She thought her heart might burst from the love that swelled forth.

"I've traveled enough, my love," she uttered quietly. "Let's go home."

4/9